RADIO SIGA

T0030416

Sandorf Passage books are available to the
trade through Independent Publishers Group:
ipgbook.com | (800) 888-4741.

Library of Congress Control Number:
2021952114

ISBN: 978-9-53351-370-6

This Book is published with financial support by
the Republic of Croatia's Ministry of Culture and Media.

RADIO SIGA
IVAN VIDAK

TRANSLATED BY MATT ROBINSON

SAN-
DORF
PAS-
SAGE

SOUTH PORTLAND | MAINE

1.

IT IS A DAUNTING and thankless task to identify the causes and describe the nature of the unusual laziness of Kalman Gubica. Even today, it seems as if this almost primeval character trait, devoured for centuries by the burden that comes with being one of the seven deadly sins, cannot escape narrow-minded and wholly oversimplified interpretation. In this, many forget that a person toils not only with hands and feet but also with the head, and that it is precisely this unseen labor that is not uncommonly held aloft as the crowning achievement of the entire glorious history of the human race. Many of those who have spent small eternities looking at the sky, at the earth, at fire or water, squeezing out a few bright fragments from an otherwise turbid and unclear picture, are often, like Kalman, branded plain lazy in their own communities, grasshoppers happily making music under the summer sun while the hard-working ants, bathed in sweat, curse their own bitter fate. True, Kalman was no philosopher, no stargazer. He was not a thinker of any kind. But nor was he a parasite. He scornfully dismissed the lesson of that tendentious fable he once heard from Father Pijuković. Let it be known that not one winter did Kalman Gubica go to his neighbor asking to share a meal or a little firewood. Besides, a strange sense of pride and dignity, which Kalman had in grotesque proportions, did not permit him to demean himself before anyone, at least not consciously or of his own free will. The source of that ravenous dignity lay precisely in the desperate poverty into which Kalman was born, like almost every other resident of Siga, since it is well-known that poverty, out of the whole spectrum of woes, frequently hits hardest precisely at the dignity of man.

Kalman Gubica was born a bastard child in the year 1920, in Siga. Already "getting on a bit" at the age of 27, his mother, Marta Gubica, was corrupted by one Lajos Kőrösi, an outsider from Hungary. This Kőrösi had fled his country in 1919, having taken an active part in the Béla Kun revolution. Defectors at that time were being sought by the Yugoslav authorities, and Kőrösi spent an entire year hiding out in the village. Fortunately, among the poor of Siga there were many who sympathized with the ideals of socialism, and Kőrösi did not want for water, food, or a roof over his head. And since in the village there was no real repressive law enforcement—the six police officers and their sergeant were not particularly enterprising—Kőrösi even worked the fields, helping those who had helped him. This was apparently where Marta met him. In the fields. There were no witnesses to their relationship. No one ever saw them alone. But one day, at dawn, as Kőrösi and several others were getting ready to travel to America and were loading their meager belongings onto a wagon, Marta, already visibly pregnant and therefore branded by society, approached and took his hand. Sándor Kis, who happened upon them and translated their parting—since Kőrösi and Marta were unable to communicate particularly well with words—would later say that the Hungarian had promised he would send someone to get her as soon as he got settled, or at least send her the money for the journey. Marta quietly bade him farewell and, before the sun was too hot, carefully returned home, where another wagon was waiting to take the mother-to-be to the fields. A few months later, Kalman was born. In the family home of his mother, who at that time lived with her parents, his arrival was the cause of little commotion. Marta's parents, already elderly, were pleased with the offspring and swallowed the slight unease caused by the illegitimacy of the child. It would appear that America also swallowed Kőrösi, since he was never heard of again. Marta never spoke of it to anyone; she became withdrawn and went to work as a day laborer on the Baranja plains. She would travel on Sunday afternoons and only return early in the evening of the following Saturday; the next day she would leave again. It started when Kalman was eight months old and, in a way, never stopped. Aged four, Kalman saw his mother for the last time one Sunday afternoon. He was agitated and pleading for her to stay, so she made him yet another cup of poppy tea and saw him off to sleep. She never again returned from the Baranja plains, and no one could say with any certainty what had happened. Those from Siga who worked with her recalled that she was still with them on the Friday. However, on the Saturday, the day she was supposed to return home, Marta was nowhere to be seen. All manner of stories did the rounds in Siga: that Kőrösi had finally sent for her or that he had even come himself, that she had run off with a foreman from the plains, that someone had killed her when she had refused to give herself to him, that she was dead precisely because she had given herself, that she had fled and was hiding with the outlaw Čaruga. People said all sorts of things, but no one knew the truth. In the end, it remained a mystery. To this day, the only indisputable fact is that Marta was never seen again in Siga. For the people of the village, her story served to frighten disobedient children, particularly girls. "You'll end up like that Marta Gubica!" they would say, as if there was little doubt she had indeed suffered a dire fate. The only person whom the story really frightened was Kalman.

Kalman had only vague memories of those first four years of life with his mother, the odd picture that would flash before his eyes. This is of course understandable given his age, even if we know that Marta spent a good part of the winter in Siga, since at that time there was not enough work on the plains to go around. Still, even had he been older, he would not have remembered those winters due to the sheer amount of poppy tea Marta gave him, even by village standards. There was not a single family in Siga that did not partake of that distinctive, foul-tasting drink. Rare was the child who was not given poppy tea at least once in early childhood to calm them down, put them to sleep, or simply "immobilize" them for a certain period when there was something the adults had to do and the child was getting in the way or there was no one to look after them. Old Father Paja Kujundžić testified as much: "Old faces there are many in Siga, but long lives are few, the cause of which, in my humble opinion, is that life for these people begins early. In these times, since the grazing has gone and the poverty grown, work begins too soon. But the most dangerous cause is poison. The strong rakija they drink contaminates their lives. Thus the development of the body lags; it is not possible to regularly maintain one's health and fully develop one's body, which the mother is already poisoning with rakija in the womb, continuing after birth with the 'elixir of sleep,' and, when grown up, rakija again until the grave." In those days of worry over their missing daughter, Grandma and Grandpa stopped brewing Kalman the elixir of sleep, and his intense restlessness seemed to them justified under the circumstances. However, when little Kalman fell into a terrifying fever, which at times bore the characteristics of complete madness, they had no choice but to call Doctor Michael Deitsch, who announced that the fever would last about a month and told them that, after the symptoms had passed and the medicine he left was finished, not even in a fit of insanity should they give the child poppy tea. And sure enough, after a month, Kalman calmly left his bed and became a quiet, pensive, slightly nervous child.

Village life leaves little time for mourning. The struggle for bare survival forces people to leave the past behind without much hesitation, to cling by the skin of their teeth to time's coattails, dragging them inexorably into tomorrow. But one must hold on hard, furiously, until the teeth begin to crack and one loses one's strength. And when that happens, one must remain calm, not lose one's head. Just like Kalman's grandpa when he suffered a heart attack in the fields a year after Marta's disappearance. A man who had worked tirelessly from the age of seven, knocked to the ground one hot August, face down in the dry, sandy earth. Several men leapt to his aid, but there was nothing that could be done. They simply turned him onto his back and watched how his big cloudy eyes grew moist and widened on his dusty face, how his grunts of pain grew less frequent, shallower, and, finally, his gaze froze somewhere up high in the bright blue firmament above him. He was only fifty, but that was a respectable age for Siga at that time, when both body and soul had already had enough after just five decades. Though it was customary for men to take much younger wives, Kalman's grandma and grandpa were the same age.

Of course, their daughter's disappearance scarred Grandma deeply too, but her grandchild was of great solace. She too began day laboring—but only locally, in Siga, like Grandpa had done—and tried to raise her grandchild as best she could. She would wake in the middle of the night and, by candlelight, prepare the food for that day before the cockerel had crowed. Then she would leave for the fields and return in the early evening. Kalman would wake with the first light, get out of bed, wash with water in a bowl prepared for him by his grandma, and head into the yard to feed the animals with his small, clumsy hands. Then all that remained of his morning duties was to open the gate and let out the ducks onto the Old Danube. It was enough to let those strange feathered creatures out into the street; they found their own way to the Old Danube riverbed. They stayed there all day long and returned in the evening, waddling together to the gate, when all that was left was to let them in. Sometimes Kalman, by now five years old, was unable to close the gate after the ducks had departed and would ask for help from his elderly neighbor, Eva, left behind to cook after the rest of her family had gone to work. Kalman had the remainder of the day to himself. At that point, the street did not hold much appeal, since the house and yard were such an endless source of wonder. The yard was divided into two parts: the first stretching the length of the house, with a small patch of clover and a well; the second part behind the house, separated by a wooden fence and where there were fruit trees, vegetables, and a tiny patch of corn. First, with a feeling of immense satisfaction, he would walk through the clover that bordered an earthen plateau around the fenced well, which was covered with a few wooden planks on which were stacked large stones so that Kalman could not lift them. He would drive out of the clover any flying creature that might be hiding there before heading to the other part of the yard, the kitchen garden, and checking with curiosity how much things had grown. A five-year-old child might be expected to leave a mess in his wake, but Kalman was the exact opposite of what might be expected. He trod lightly wherever he went, made sure to put back everything exactly where he had found it, and, in general, demonstrated a particularly refined sense of order. He would behave the same way inside the house. In the fields, Grandma boasted a little uncertainly—fearing that it might, in fact, be a cause for concern—that it was as if her grandson hovered above the ground. The earth beneath the "carpet"—old sacks, torn up and washed, or patchwork rugs sewn together from worn-out and discarded clothes— and the thin layer of lime on top were exactly as she had left them in the morning (she had checked!), so the only explanation was that the child either sat very still or floated above the ground, which would always amuse those around her. Kalman would slip between the modest furniture to the long planks that served as beds, leaning against the wall by the stove, and sit on the quilt that was stuffed with corn husks and look long and quietly around himself with an unusual degree of attention, as if listening to something that no one else could hear. In winter, life was organized a little differently, for good reason. For a start, Grandma did not go into the fields but would put her loom to work, supplying the whole of Church Street with fabric for upholstery, shirts, underwear, and other such essentials. Kalman, despite the cold and exposure that winter brought, all the same spent much of the day in the yard, before calmly, drowsily watching Grandma's loom from that same plank and quilt, until he succumbed to sleep.

When he turned seven, it came time for Kalman to be enrolled in school. In many ways this was a momentous event in Kalman's young life. Because of his somewhat specific family circumstances, but also his distinctive character, up until he was seven Kalman did not have a particularly rich social life. He was cursorily acquainted with a few boys on his street; their encounters, so rare that he knew little more than their names, were marked by a degree of mistrust. His reputation did not help: the Hungarian bastard who lived with his grandma, who took no interest in the things that any healthy schoolkid should be interested in—like fishing, falconry, fighting, and a host of others capers that are in principle undesirable yet expected, and the absence of which is a cause of concern for parents—and, in general, did nothing to advance his position in society. However, in a relatively short period of time that position was, to a degree, corrected through school. "To a degree," because we cannot say that he became particularly popular. To many he remained plain odd, but he succeeded in being accepted by a few classmates. Alas, the worst ones: those made to repeat a year, future delinquents and horse thieves. That small social step forward would not translate into longer-lasting friendship; in the future he would only say hello to these young people in the street, but it allowed him to pass through this institution at least marginally accepted, and considering the reputation and status of the boys he associated with in school, it would spare him any beating he may have otherwise been dealt. As a student, Kalman demonstrated certain signs of brightness. But that is where the impression left on the teacher ended, since it was right about that time that his tendency for laziness began to show. It was as if he understood everything with ease, but moved not even a millimeter from that point, since he could never get to grips with learning and remembering under pressure of obligation. He developed an intense resistance to all forms of direction, examination, or attempts to discipline him, so that already in his first days of school he crossed swords several times with his teacher, Milan Stojšić. Fortunately, Mima (as he was known in Siga) on the whole turned a blind eye—even showed some sympathy—because he appreciated Kalman's otherwise sharp, authentic, and, ultimately, uncorrupted mind.

The winter spanning 1928 and 1929 was one of the coldest that even the oldest residents of Siga could recall. That January, as dictatorship was taking hold in the old kingdom and Kalman attended second grade, temperatures fell to minus 27 degrees. For two whole months everything was frozen; people crossed the Danube—the real one—by horse-drawn cart as if crossing a field, worried hunters left food for game in forest feeders, snow refused to muddy and melt, and time seemed to stand still. One of those January days on his return from school, Kalman found his grandma sitting in the yard, leaning against the round wall of the well. Her eyes were shut, her head hung loosely toward her right shoulder, and frost had formed on her eyebrows, her lashes, and her thin, downy mustache. And so, that cold winter of 1929, Kalman found himself alone.

That a child might be left without a single close family member—often even without an extended family member—was nothing new for Siga. At that time, death came often and early and seemed to be a far more integral part of human life than it is today, when it is often viewed as a foreign, almost inhuman event lurking in the dark at the end of a path. At that time, people were still dying of tuberculosis, the occasional cholera epidemic, malnutrition, exhaustion, and all sorts of other ills. Of course, alcohol took lives too. And all those deaths inevitably left behind young children, all alone. Care for them fell to the Orphanage Father, the person whom the village warden and his attendants appointed guardian of the orphans. The whole of Siga would collect food for these children, and every day the Orphanage Father would distribute it (prepared with the help of some women), while also taking care of their other needs, such as making sure they regularly attended school. Those children who inherited houses and were not too young to live alone in them remained in their homes. Those who were too young were taken in by willing families or went into the poorhouse, an institution—really nothing more than an ordinary house—in which were accommodated all those, young or old, who had been left with no better option. Kalman was a borderline case. Though, at not yet nine years old, he was too young to live alone, Anton Klet, the Orphanage Father at that time, had heard from his Aunt Eva, Kalman's neighbor, that the little boy had been used to being alone for some time and that she was ready to help out whenever required, the same as she had done till then. And so Kalman was allowed to remain in his family home, with daily contact with Eva (known across Siga as Nanny Eva), who offered to cook for him as long as the groceries were provided, and with visits from Anton Klet himself, who came once or twice a week. It should be noted that there were some distant relatives, but they were deaf to Anton's appeals for help, most likely out of fear of starvation.

Besides a handful of landowners and a few artisans and traders, most people in Siga ate the same humble food as Anton's orphans, which made life easier for the kitchen ladies and relieved them of the headache of having to answer every day the question of what to cook. So Monday was Lenten potatoes and (dry) Lenten sweet bread; Tuesday was beans without roux; Wednesday was fried mashed potatoes and pasta with potato stew; Thursday was potatoes and pork pie; Friday was pureed beans without roux; Saturday was bread soup and semolina noodles; and Sunday was chicken stew ("pretty stew") with noodles or meat in vinegar. Or on Sunday they simply cooked beans again, this time with roux.

Sticking to the routines of nutrition and school, as well as being able to remain in his own home, helped soften the loss of the last member of Kalman's family. Anton and everyone else with whom Kalman was in touch were surprised by his stoicism.

At his grandma's funeral, for example, unlike at his grandpa's, Kalman did not shed a tear or make a sound, and people were already talking about "poor Kalman" who had been through such unhappiness even before his first decade was out, whose "tears had dried up," his "heart had been broken," and much else besides. Everything could be described with a few stock phrases saved up for moments of great misfortune.

This living arrangement remained largely unchanged until Kalman finished his four years of school. As a prize for finishing, teacher Mima took all the school-leavers to the cinema owned by Nikola Bešlin, a local trader who had turned one of his buildings into a movie theater after buying a projector in Vienna. Plain wooden chairs were arranged in ten rows, of which the first two that evening were reserved for the school-leavers. Against the wall to the right, on chairs separated from the rest, sat four firemen, while on the left, right up close to the screen, an organ had been installed at which sat the church cantor, Rotlander. The school-leavers took their places in the half dark, the other rows having long ago been filled by the other interested people of Siga, and within a few minutes there was total darkness and the distant, quiet hum of the fuel generator somewhere in the yard producing electricity. This was all soon engulfed by the terrifying sound of the organ accompanying the moving lights on the large screen, and the whole thing resembled some kind of Mass; the cantor didn't know any other songs, so he played the same ones he played in church. Since the advent of film in Siga, the villagers had become accustomed mainly to those of Charlie Chaplin and Harry Piel, so when, with the organ in accompaniment, *The Cabinet of Dr. Caligari* began to roll before their eyes, they were in complete shock. No one left the projection. Films were still a fascinating phenomenon. But most of those present shifted nervously in their seats and occasionally turned their heads or covered their eyes with their hands. "Jesus Mary," a few women whispered, pulling their legs together further beneath the chairs. The children, in general, broke the tension with loud cries but were shushed by their parents. In any case, word quickly spread through the village about a strangely terrifying film, and almost everyone wanted to watch it, even if only out of simple curiosity. This resulted in pleas to Father Pijuković for Mass to be held for a time without the organ, because its sound reminded the frightened people of Siga of their chilling experience at the movie house. For the rest of the summer, the streets at night were emptier than usual, while some innkeepers locked their doors at sunset, which all in fact says more about the state of mind of those who lived in Siga at the time than about the influence of German expressionism.

The film left a deep impression on Kalman. In fairness, it was not that he found it as chilling as most in Siga, though there was an element of that too, as much as he felt an intense fascination with what the film had revealed. Is that really Germany? If so, what other horrifying wonders is the rest of the world hiding? What lives out there on the great map that teacher Mima had laid out before them?

The house that Kalman inherited, and particularly the yard, quickly underwent dramatic changes. Many might again attribute it to laziness and indifference, but for some reason Kalman took great satisfaction in observing how nature took over the large divided yard, how everything was transformed into a dense jungle in which Kalman saw a profusion of life, shade, and peace, and everyone else saw little more than an unruly mess. The only gardening that took place in that wilderness was around the short, narrow, crooked brick path that led from the gate to the entrance of the house. When chloroplast life would emerge in the space between the bricks and hinder his walk along the path, Kalman would pull out enough plants to allow unobstructed passage. Sometimes he might sit for hours on the open veranda, watching that quiet life and sensing how the peace was filling him up like cold boza on a summer's day. That's how he spent the whole of that graduation summer, until Anton Klet brought him back down to earth in the autumn.

One cold Sunday at the end of November 1931, Kalman was visited by Anton and Father Pijuković. It was spelled out to him that he was no longer quite so young and helpless, that the institution of the Orphanage Father could not feed him forever, and that it was about time he found work. They counseled against an apprenticeship since it would mean going without an income for at least another three years, and when it would finish he was unlikely to have an easy time because many handymen and tradesmen were without work. They were relieved when they saw that Kalman had no interest whatsoever in becoming an artisan. Then they concluded that at eleven years old he was perhaps still too young for a full day's work in the fields, so day labor was still out of the question, as far as they were concerned, although it was not unheard of for young children. But, times had changed. Paying no heed to Kalman's decisive "that's not for me," Father Pijuković came out with a proposal that had obviously been prepared in advance. Namely, since cantor Rotlander, clearly insulted by the organ being cut from Mass after *The Cabinet of Dr. Caligari*, had left Siga in protest, the position of church cantor had been left empty. And Father Pijuković had happened to recall the intelligence Kalman had displayed during religious studies, and so offered to personally teach him to play a number of simple, spiritual organ compositions so that he could become the new cantor. Of course, if it proved a good idea and Kalman demonstrated a knack, interest, and commitment, well, he could go far. Kalman was, in principle, interested in the idea, but Father Pijuković quickly realized the sheer naïveté of his intention after the first few practice sessions in the church. For a start, Kalman displayed an overwhelming lack of talent. And when Pijuković recalled his own agony learning to play the organ, he even felt a degree of shame for his thoughtlessness and completely unfounded ambition. So he quickly dismissed Kalman from the post and gave him enough money to get through the winter. That is, he gave the money to Anton, who eagerly accepted, and the question of Kalman's employment was not brought up again until the spring.

Kalman spent the winter wandering around the frozen outdoors, getting to know for the first time the wider surroundings of his birthplace. People watched in bewilderment as this child roamed the district alone, sometimes even worriedly offering him help or a lift in their carts. Most times he would wave them away and mumble grumpily, because people were spoiling his experience, pressing on briskly toward some imagined destination. On those walks his attention would be drawn most of all to the life playing out along the Old Danube, like a separate entity on the edge of the community, with its own rules, rhythm, and habits. Until 1902, Siga was a settlement on the banks of the Danube. There, the river took a turn and dropped down from the main course (north-south) some five kilometers east, like a breast on the top of which sat the settlement of Siga—the nipple. But maintenance work between 1898 and 1902 saw a new branch of the Danube dug out through Blaževica and Kalandoš, which ran eleven and a half kilometers and cut off the old bend, the breast of Siga, sparing the settlement from flooding but depriving it of direct contact with the Danube. For a time, river traffic still took the old route, until roughly 1910, after which boats became an increasingly rare sight before disappearing almost completely. Some cargo traffic did remain, particularly boats carrying wood from the forests across the Old Danube and barges transporting wheat. The water mills hung on the longest; two would remain in use right up until the middle of the century. Ever since, the space between the old and new Danube riverbeds has been crisscrossed by a host of channels and tunnels, so that the Old Danube beneath the village will be severed more and more from the new course and force of the water; as a consequence, the whole of this area will become marshland. But in Kalman's time, the social life along the Old Danube was rich. All the people of the river would gather at the old quay in Dola, which from 1872 was also equipped to receive passenger traffic, and, for that very purpose, a tavern called Tench was built. Water millers and those who used their services—fishermen, bargemen, ferrymen, shipyard workers—all gathered in the Tench. These were people who happily spurned the "refined" world of the village inns of which there were many in

Siga, choosing instead the already quite decadent Tench as their place of relaxation and socializing. They were not bothered by the many troublemakers, shady traders, and smugglers who had picked the same tavern for their own get-togethers. Minding one's own business was most important. Even the police steered clear, ever since one of their number was stabbed to death in 1923 following a game of blackjack.

Kalman became closely acquainted with the Danube basin in the spring of 1932, when Anton Klet proposed to have him hired as a kurtalaš. A kurtala was a towrope used to pull the old river barges and cargo boats. For example, somewhere on one side of the Old Danube a barge would be loaded up with timber and have to be pulled by ropes to the other side, then along the bank all the way to the quay at Dola. The barge would be pulled by people or horses, but whichever it was, someone—the kurtalaš—would every now and again have to lift the towrope with a long, forked pole to stop it snagging on the bushes and tree stumps along the bank. Kalman accepted the offer more out of a longing for the water than the job itself. But he gave up after the first day, as much out of laziness as for more objective reasons, since to lift the towrope required at least a degree of strength and patience, and he could not pride himself on either. That first day, after the last barge was moored, the workers invited him for a drink at Tench and, with smiles of approval, watched as he experienced the shock of his first glass of rakija. They patted him on the shoulder after his baptism of fire and were more than a little surprised when he failed to turn up for work the next day. But the real surprise followed that afternoon, when they came across Kalman in the Tench, sitting at a table with a glass of rakija in front of him. The workman who, without much complaint, had lifted the towrope that day instead of Kalman grabbed him by the collar and threw him outside, to the sniggering of everyone present and the observation that there was no place in the Tench for snot-nosed kids and layabouts. Enraged, Kalman ran home red cheeked, locked the gate behind him, and spent three days licking his wounds in shame. He expected Anton to turn up that very day and lecture him, but he didn't. Only Eva came around, bearing food but no questions. After three days, Kalman returned to Dola and asked the workers to take him back. They coldly refused.

In a way, that event severed Kalman from the carefreeness of youth, if his youth had ever been without a care. That whole summer Kalman somewhat ruefully sought a way, a purpose and a justification to spend time on the water. He pleaded with the millers and the impoverished fishermen to grant him work, which they sometimes did, but only temporarily, one job to the next, since few could afford constant paid help. Those who could had long ago hired people of trust. Who would take a risk on a boy of barely eleven years old who had already demonstrated his fickle nature to the ferrymen and bargemen? From time to time they would let him transfer the odd sack of flour, put a catch of fish in storage, sweep up, chop and stack wood—but it was all, as they say, short-lived, and paid a pittance. This futile, hand-to-mouth existence was Kalman's routine right up until that winter. When what little work he had disappeared due to the cold and snow—because of which he started slowly to despair, since, besides being on the water, he liked the impermanence of such employment as well as the freedom that it brought—a new opportunity presented itself. Every winter the municipality hired people, usually Gypsies or the most destitute, to collect ice for the municipal ice cellar. They would cut it or break it up from the Old Danube or one of the flooded ditches that were all over the district since the course of the river had changed, and transport it to the ice cellar by wagon or sledge. This ice brought the Siga authorities a handsome income during the summer, when they would sell it to butchers and innkeepers. It was for this that Anton once more thought of Kalman. He sensed a headache coming on because of that boy. On the one hand, it was clear to him that there could be problems with Kalman and that he would have a far harder time sending him on his way than any other orphan, but on the other, the whole thing had in a way been privatized since Eva had personally interceded on behalf of the little one and begged Anton to do everything possible to help him. Given that Kalman had shown an interest in life on the water, work with ice seemed to Anton an ideal opportunity. And Kalman indeed took great satisfaction in collecting ice, and when, on the very first day after work was done, he and a group of Gypsies stopped for a drink at the Tench—where those present would first size up newcomers, whoever walked in the door, and then disinterestedly return to their conversations and glasses, and in that way consent to their entrance—Kalman considered his triumph complete. That day he got drunk for the first time, and threw up until late in the night, but all the same was at the agreed spot at the crack of dawn and did not allow his hangover to influence his effectiveness on the job. That was his life for the next four years, until he turned sixteen: scrounging for day labor in the summer and breaking ice in the winter. In fairness, it is worth admitting that, since he had been granted entry to the Tench, he somehow came across summer work more easily, for which he could thank the fact that the people of the river had, in a sense, accepted him.

It was at this time that some of Kalman's character traits, about which we have already spoken, became fully developed, but some quite new ones also appeared. One should not be fooled into thinking his employment had cured him of his laziness. In fact, everything else in his life suffered from a habitual lack of resolve to get anything done: to maintain the house and grounds, patch up his worn-out clothes, consider his circumstances and come up with any kind of plan. That said, Kalman would often embark on a task, but would quickly come to the conclusion that it could not be done properly and so would set it aside unfinished, since who in their right mind wants something done the wrong way? Perhaps it was the accumulation of those quite distinctive but not at all benign frustrations that come with being a lazy perfectionist that resulted in the basic manifestation of a core characteristic: arrogance. On arrival in the world of adulthood, Kalman could be best described as an arrogant ignoramus. Although, as we know, he was indeed bright, but he invested almost nothing in his brightness, except for a particular self-regard and, later, a belief that it was precisely he who understood everything and that everyone else could only dream of such intelligence. That comfortable position gradually developed and reached its peak at the end of Kalman's adolescence. Arrogance and an uncompromising sense of self-regard were his main social weapons. We can only speculate when it comes to the fear and catastrophic deficit of self-confidence that stood behind everything. However, it was fascinating to see how people unquestioningly accepted what was served up to them, and how many over time developed a respect for and sense of awe toward that loud and disagreeable young man.

To this character diagnosis was added a kind of identity annex when his neighbor Eva for the first time explained who exactly his father was, the Hungarian socialist Lajos Kőrösi, and planted within him a certain national self-awareness by teaching him Hungarian. Although conscious of the ethnicity of his mother and her side of the family, Kalman happily accepted this fact, since it was news and gave him scope to interpret himself in fresh and ever new ways through contemplation of the mystical figure of his father and his unknown fate. Knowledge of the Hungarian language is a question of self-respect for any member of this people living in the diaspora. In the nearby village of Bezdan, and particularly in Kupusina, there live entire generations who to this day have not learned a word of this, our language, and know solely to speak Hungarian. In Siga such cases were exceptionally rare, despite the fact that every Hungarian family within its own four walls spoke only Hungarian. That knowledge of Hungarian would prove extremely useful to Kalman at the time of the Hungarian occupation of Bačka during World War II.

And here we are, at last, in the autumn of 1936, when sixteen-year-old Kalman Gubica entered into the employment that would leave an indelible mark on the rest of his life and determine his destiny. Until that moment, the job of town drummer, as it was known in Siga, was held by Mata Šimunov. But that autumn Mata took to his sickbed, from which he was soon taken to his grave. That very moment, Anton, in the hope of forever relieving the pressure placed on him by Nanny Eva, thought of Kalman and decided to do everything to have him hired in Mata's place. First he went to the village warden, a post held at that time by Stipan Francuz, and pledged his good standing on behalf of Kalman, so that the warden would agree to install the lad in a job that was most often for life. Town drummers, at least those who were picked to do the job, were always, to a man, eccentrics. To successfully adapt to the job, a person was required to possess a degree of almost theatrical thirst for showing off and the vanity that comes with it. That thirst and vanity were vital in order to cultivate desire and appetite in the town drummer. An uncompromising, powerful desire and determination, which cannot be without foundation, without substance, and which would drive the town drummer to visit the twelve village crossroads, bang the drum and call out the news when drunk, sick, tired, and sleepy, come rain, snow, frost, and searing heat. The warden came around to the idea relatively easily, and it remained only for Anton to convince Kalman, and that would be, he reasoned, a simple task, since that young one was hungry for renown, like a disinherited son convinced he has been fatefully wronged, that the world owes him, who is ready to do anything in order to take what, in his mind, belongs to him. And Anton was right. At first, Kalman thought a little, furrowing his brow. But when Anton, correctly reading his thoughts, said that nothing would stop him from frequenting the Tench in his free time, Kalman brightened

IVAN VIDAK

up, became even childishly excited, and started to pace up and down, electrified. He pulled at his hair, giggled with satisfaction, gripped Anton's hand, and then even embraced him before running to the Tench to announce his great, unexpected success. He opened the door with a bang and without hesitation, forefinger raised, headed straight toward the tavern keeper, Öcsike, and requested that he open him a tab so he could buy the whole place a round. Once it had been explained to him, Öcsike put up little resistance, since the job of town drummer brought in a sure and tidy income, so there was not much danger that the debt would not be paid. Of course, a town drummer's salary was not such that a person could get rich, buy a house, or simply accumulate any significant sum, but in the company of the poor and humble peasant who was often no stranger to hunger, a solid and regular sum of money was no less than a fortune. Kalman drank wantonly all night, bought rounds for friend and foe, and celebrated himself without inhibition, roused in part by alcohol, in part by his new social status. He feared no one because he was now part of the powers that be—at the very edge of that constellation, but nevertheless important enough to enjoy the protection of the sergeant and his six coppers, the same as any other official. At one point he sat in the middle of the Tench and practically wept with happiness. He looked around at all those terrifying faces that had instilled in him such fear: bearded, toothless, murky faces, and the even more terrifying faces of the smugglers, shaven and cold, the expressionless faces of a few crippled veterans of World War I, the wily faces of river captains, and the awkward and ominously grimacing faces of the troublemakers who would sometimes stop by before disappearing for months and about whom no one knew anything. To Kalman, they were all now just a collection of screwed-up masks that posed no threat to him anymore.

The first day, sickeningly hungover, he failed to even turn up for work, even though waiting for him in the municipality building were Anton and old town drummer, Marko Kolar, who was blessed, or cursed, with such an unusually long life that after retiring he was made to train not only his own successor, the late Mata Šimunov, but his successor's successor too. But thanks to Anton's inexhaustible goodwill, this incident was also ironed out, and Kalman became the town drummer after all. Predictably or not, he proved highly talented in his new job, and the training was unusually short. At least, that may have been Kalman's own subjective reading of the situation, since after three days of lessons he had already assumed a presumptuous attitude toward his elderly teacher, who could hardly wait for those first signs of capriciousness to withdraw to the safe routines of old age. Nevertheless, Kalman's performance could not be faulted. He was loud, clear, and stirring and had a tendency to improvise that was all his own, meaning he had a habit of appending to the daily news a comment or two of his own making. For example:

Hear ye, hear ye!

Bakers ordered to cut the price of bread from three dinars to two and a half.

Health service report says that in Siga our wells are too shallow. It is decided we need thirty-five Norton wells between eighteen and twenty-three meters deep.

Then, with a slightly different, warmer intonation, he would add cheekily:

All that remains is to decide who's going to dig 'em!

Then he would mount his bicycle and head off to the eleven remaining crossroads, losing not an ounce of enthusiasm or élan, and delivering his proclamations always with the same fervor. He struggled with the drumming to begin with. Although he was told he need not wear himself out, that it was enough to hit it a few times, he would practice all day to produce a rhythmically correct drumroll, which after all required a little practice and good coordination. He would drum in his yard, pompously parading and demonstrating a hitherto unseen determination and resolve. Indeed, even though at the start he made many mistakes, not once did he get upset or give up on the whole thing, spitting out profanities. Quickly and with ease he moved on from his failures, always starting over, untiringly —almost with a smile—until he achieved a proper, fast, and clear sound on the drum.

The bicycle was another element of Kalman's new employment that brought with it a whiff of glamour, for that bicycle, the Village Hall bicycle, was the only one in Siga. Perhaps Vámoser or some other landowner had a bicycle on his estate, but for sure no one in Vámoser's family, and certainly not he himself, paraded the muddy or dusty streets of Siga on it. And since the former town drummer, Mata, had been uninterested in and even scared by the bicycle, Kalman became the first and only presence to race around the village on that noble contraption. In fairness, it took a few days and a couple of painful bruises before he had mastered cycling, but again it did not occur to him to give up. Very quickly he felt free enough that he stopped returning the bicycle to the Village Hall after work was done and was constantly in the saddle, drunk or sober, day or night.

In those first few months of employment, Kalman won an inseparable friend, completely by chance and thanks to his bicycle: a dog he would call Toza. This, at that point, unnamed stray, one of many in Siga, one day quietly joined Kalman on his ride. He bounded along beside him and gazed with fascination at this human being on two wheels zigzagging down the road, struggling to keep his balance (completely sober!) and clumsily clutching the handlebars, yet all the same strangely moving forward. Kalman tried a few times to shoo the dog away, and twice even got off his bicycle and charged at him, but Toza did not give in. He did not appear at all scared. He was so impressed by the bicycle that he retreated a few meters and then came back and continued following. As soon as Kalman became more adept and rode faster, Toza's interest grew. He was no longer strolling after an unskilled rider, but could really stretch his legs, which made the whole thing even more fun. After those initial, unsuccessful attempts at chasing him away, Kalman decided he would simply ignore him. In the morning, the dog would be waiting for him at the gate, but Kalman would not even look at him, just get on his bicycle and set about his business. He stopped looking back, although he knew very well that Toza was following him; when he would stop at a crossroads and beat his drum, the dog would calmly sit or lie down next to the bicycle and watch, waiting for the little performance to finish. And when, after work was done, he would stop by the Tench and leave the bicycle leaning against a nearby poplar tree, Toza would again lie down next to the bicycle and wait until Kalman stumbled out of the tavern at some ungodly hour. He would often be so drunk that he would have to push the bicycle, but that would not dent Toza's dedication, and he would walk along beside the bicycle all the same, glancing up occasionally at Kalman until the gate was closed in front of him. Toza would then sit, shift nervously a few times, yawn, curl up against the gate, and fall asleep. They would repeat the ritual the following day. And that's how things remained until January 1937. The event that altered their relationship played out one cold night as Kalman led a drunken discussion in the Tench. He had just made another of the pompous, dramatic pauses he so liked, when from outside came a loud bark, a growling mixed with a panicked human cry. Confused, everyone went outside and saw Toza, a trouser leg in his jaws, sitting quite calmly next to the bicycle and looking at Kalman. The bicycle itself was on the ground a few meters from the trunk of the poplar against which Kalman, as usual, had leaned it. Toza received a large portion of goulash, as a symbol of recognition and acceptance, as well as a guardian and a place in Kalman's home, right next to the bed, which only goes to show how terrified Kalman had been at the prospect of losing that practical means of transport. And so that village novelty—a fresh, young town drummer on a bicycle, dog in tow—gradually became one more ordinary part of the everyday lives of the people of Siga.

It remains only to mention the event that would play a significant role in Kalman's already somewhat disjointed mental development, and which is part of the period of innocence, before the great ruptures that would afflict Kalman and much of the world. It happened on June 29, 1939, the day of the village fête. There is something so debauched about that day, so over-the-top, that by late evening, people, mainly the men, are no longer recognizable. Everything begins with Mass, as is customary, given it is a religious day. But even then, before returning home for lunch, the drinking begins in the inn. After lunch, in the late afternoon, everyone heads to the tents with live music next to the football field, to the carousels, halvah stalls, and confectionary. The women and children stick to that innocuous part of the program, eating ice cream, drinking lemonade and cordials. The grown men toss rings onto bottles, shoot tin cans, play cards, or visit those illusionists who make you guess under which of three thimbles they have hidden a single grain. But they usually end up in one of the ten spacious tents, drinking hard liquor, eating, and reveling to the music. The evening program is announced in the afternoon: theater and movie shows, circus acts, and that year something special—a performance by the Sombor strongman István Pista Nagy. On a simple, slow-moving village wagon stood Nagy, dressed in a comically tight costume, flexing his muscles and every now and again bending an iron bar. Every ten minutes, an assistant who stood next to him would smash a rock on Nagy's head with a fairly large hammer. Next to the wagon walked Kalman, pompously banging his drum and announcing, "Tonight in Siga, Pista Nagy, the strongman of Sombor, wrestling champion of the Balkans, participant in the Berlin Olympics, will show what he can do. Line up, people, line up! Only one dinar!"

Kalman himself, however, did not go to watch Pista Nagy that evening. Initially he planned to go to the movie projection, but then it was announced at the last moment that a troupe from Germany would perform in Kata Lorbach's inn. The mystical call of the theater was like a magnet to Kalman. Film had its limitations, but a theater performance was the height of splendor: live actors, sweat beading on their foreheads, the smell, the cracking of joints, the panting and sniffing, not to mention the quality of live speech! The situation with the Germans was already difficult. Though in Siga there had not been any significant friction, and most of the Germans were not easily impressed by German National Socialism, one group gathered around the local Kulturbund identified with its vision. Kata Lorbach's inn was precisely the place where such people who were members of this cultural and political organization, frequently bearing Nazi symbols, came together and celebrated themselves. It is unclear to what extent Kata Lorbach herself believed in the new ideology of the Reich, but her husband, innkeeper Johan Lorbach, had already answered the call of the fatherland a year earlier and in all probability was by then picking up military knowledge in one of the Schutzstaffel training centers. He would disappear somewhere on the Eastern Front in the winter of 1941. Kata was a stocky but well-proportioned and enchanting woman, sensual in her splendor, but strong and stern, capable and rational, and she proved a more successful innkeeper than her adventure-inclined husband with whom, in terms of romance, things had never gone well. The marriage was all but arranged; she was considerably younger than him, and they did not have children.

In Siga, ideology rarely had the potential to ignite. That handful of national-socialists who would gather at Kata's inn never became violent; at least, not before the war. The occasional chauvinistic remark was their limit, and even in those moments their non-German neighbors never took them seriously. So it was not particularly unusual that Kalman had the courage to attend a show at Kata Lorbach's. A few curious looks was about all he had to put up with before Kata gave a questioning nod in his direction, to which he briefly and clearly replied, "Beer." Kata's stern gaze stayed on him for a few more moments, particularly after she had placed a glass of beer in front of him, but then she turned around and went back to disciplining a few loud and drunk young Nazis mucking around at the bar. Kalman sipped his beer, lit a cigarette, and stared at the modest props arranged around chairs in a corner now cleared of tables for use as a stage. Two actors and three actresses quickly appeared on that improvised stage and performed a closet drama in German. Kalman understood nothing except the odd familiar Germanism that would surface out of the rolling mass of unfamiliar language that had enveloped him. The performance lasted three quarters of an hour, after which the smiling actors took their bow to loud applause and whistles from the audience. Special applause was reserved for a delicate young actress whose pretty face and porcelain skin disarmed all those present. Kalman watched and listened the whole time like an elated first communicant. After the performance, he took advantage of the excitement it had stirred and stole into the cellar of Kata's inn, which the actors were using as a dressing room. Half-naked and disheveled, the five excited actors were going wild. Kalman's presence startled them slightly. The actresses discreetly covered up their excess naked skin, but there was no sign of fear; the sight of a hypnotized fan, eyes wide open and nervously wringing his hands, only further pacified them, as if an exotic animal stood before them. Kalman was ecstatic: here they were, right in front of him, as if descended from a movie screen. Precisely the kind of different, unfathomable, and otherworldly people whose job (are they even aware?) was more or less the same as his. Using the mannerisms he had picked up poorly from films, he approached each one, a knowing look in his eye, and in the manner of a gentleman kissed their hands, the men as well as the women. The company was highly amused, and the only thing Kalman managed to hear before Kata Lorbach angrily opened the heavy wooden door was "wunderbar!" Having driven him out of the cellar, Kata did not make a scene. As soon as he was out, she stopped shouting and closed the door. That stern look, however, somehow stuck to him, and every time he met her eyes he could feel his heart in his mouth. "What the hell's wrong with me?" Kalman wondered. "Why am I scared of some busty barwoman?"

Just as he thought how much he could do with a beer right then, Kata Lorbach headed toward him with a fresh glass in her hand. Open-mouthed, Kalman took the glass, and the sight of her blue eyes looking at him from so close excited him even more; it was as if he had completely forgotten the performance and the actors, and the only thing left was to quench his thirst with freshly poured beer and sit firmly on his chair. After half an hour, he plucked up the courage to go for another beer, which Kata, from the other side of the bar, resolutely handed to him, setting down beside it a small glass of rakija, which Kalman immediately downed in front of her, accepting her game of stares without even knowing why. He returned to his table where he determined, a little awkwardly, that he had an erection. Soon the only people left in the inn besides Kalman and Kata were two quite young Nazis at the bar. At that point the almost forgotten actors emerged from the cellar, and Kata ordered the pair at the bar to take them to their lodgings, which she had arranged for them in the house of a local trader of German origin. With a smile, the Germans waved and left with the young men.

As soon as the doors were closed, Kata carefully locked them. She tucked the key into her apron and, walking toward the cellar, glanced at Kalman and said, "Come on." Panic gripped him. He cast a frightened look at the dark, threatening pit after Kata had entered the cellar and left the door open. His legs would not move. After a few moments, her head emerged from the pit and she said loudly, "What are you waiting for? Get in here!" Somehow he got up and staggered into the darkness, trying to catch his breath. Only when he entered did he realize that the darkness was not total; somewhere in the corner a kerosene lamp cast a pale light. Suddenly, Kata appeared before him, still in a skirt but her breasts bare. Big, white, round tits shone before him for the first time. He stood in front of her, completely paralyzed. He had little time to think before she took him firmly by his painfully stiff member and began to pull on it rhythmically. Helpless, his mouth open, he looked at her serious face as a small tremor coursed through his body. She released him, turned around and leaned against some wooden boxes full of empty bottles, and hitched up her skirt, showing him her round, white behind, and said, "Go on." Considering that before him stood his first sexual experience, Kalman even breathed clumsily. He approached, but she had to direct him with her hand. As soon as she began to gyrate and set the rhythm, she began moaning with satisfaction, saying, "Bastard. Filthy bastard." Although he was drowning in a flood of satisfaction and sensual ecstasy, her words sliced through Kalman like a knife. Drinking them in, he could clearly feel how the complete satisfaction of his body, intensified by the impulse of humiliation, thundered like a flood toward his testicles and disappeared somewhere in the hotness of Kata's skin. While Kata got dressed, he wiped the sweat from his brow and giggled like an imbecile. He watched her as if after a great discovery, like he was seeing her for the very first time, practically in love, ready to do anything, and did not stop sniggering. Honest and loud, satisfyingly, seductively. Kata grabbed him by the sleeve, dragged him out of the cellar, and pointed to the exit. "Out," she said. She didn't seem irritated by the laughter; in all probability she would have acted the same way if he had been somber. After she unlocked the door, he tried to kiss her, still buttoning his trousers and trying to catch his breath amid the laughter. She merely pushed him out and locked the door after him. It was dark and quiet on the street. Only the muffled, faraway sound of music. Not a soul in sight, just Toza guarding the bicycle that leaned against the tree. He lifted his head and nodded, trying to decipher, with some kind of canine intellect, the reason for the laughter that rang down the street. Kalman pushed the bicycle home that night. Toza didn't mind. He followed, constantly curious about Kalman's irrepressible giggling, and it seemed that for the first time he was more interested in the man than the bicycle.

Like many before him, Kalman paid a heavy price for lust. After that theatrical night at Kata Lorbach's, he visited her another dozen or so times. He would arrive, sit down, order a drink. Kata would serve him, but not even look at him. He would wait patiently for closing time, sitting in silence at his table and stoically putting up with the goading of a few village Nazis, who at a certain point would set off on their own shady dealings, and he would be left alone with Kata. Finally, she would call him once more into the cellar, offer up her moonlike behind and make him pay with always the same clear words: "Bastard. Filthy bastard." Then, again, with that strange mix of humiliation and satisfaction, she would throw him out onto the street without explanation. Until one day, again offering no explanation, she began throwing him out denied and not humiliated. Kalman reasoned that it was perhaps something temporary and kept coming back. But he got nothing but the drink he was served. His initial confusion turned to shock, shock into disbelief, disappointment, and grief. Eventually he stopped going to Kata's inn completely, but for a long time after, almost every night, he would ride past her window and furtively, out of the corner of his eye, peer inside.

During that time of infatuation and sexual discovery, Kalman seldom visited the Tench. He might stop by if that evening he had not planned on seeing Kata, but he would stand at the bar in silence, content to be alone, taking no part in the conversations and altercations or any kind of interaction. Everyone grew worried about him. To their inquiries he would give a confident wave of the hand, finish his drink, and leave. Later, when Kata stopped inviting him into the cellar and it was clear the end had come, he became a regular once more, still reserved, but this time without that self-confidence and serenity. Instead, there was a heavy silence about him, drinking till he hit the floor. Besides the torment of rejection, Kalman realized that Kata had awoken in him something that now refused to be put to bed. He started to chase lustfully after any number of women, with far more concrete ideas than those he had before he ever met Kata Lorbach. He began visiting local women of ill repute—Clubfoot Marica, who limped on her left leg; Sabina the Gypsy, who laid down for flour and other foodstuffs—but he struggled to rid his mind of the corpulent German. This manifested itself most obviously when morning would find him asleep at her door with no recollection of how he came to be there. She would notice him upon stepping outside to sweep up in front of the house. First, she would carefully sweep around him, and then, before leaving, empty a bucket of cold water on him. Waking up, Kalman would hear only the closing of the door as he frantically wiped the water from his face. He was tempted to believe that it was not she who had drenched him but some ill-meaning third party, but he very quickly made one of the wiser decisions of his young life—not to lie to himself about the whole situation.

In the early autumn of 1940, on the embankment along which he was returning the six kilometers from Bezdan— where in broad daylight he had visited the well-known brothel of Madam Erzsike—Kalman was caught in a terrible storm. He gripped the handlebars of the bicycle and fought to turn the pedals against the wind, while an alarmed Toza barked beside him. Somewhere near the Siga boatyard, so not far from the village, lightning lit up the sky, and the thunder became so loud that he felt his insides shudder. A few moments before the downpour began, the wind began to blow so unbearably hard that Kalman was forced to dismount and push his bicycle. He ran with it, scared and not sensing why Toza was barking ever louder and more furiously. That irritating barking didn't stop when, a few seconds later, a bolt of lightning struck Kalman directly in the head and threw him several meters from his bicycle, leaving him there, smoking, under the first drops of rain. Toza went on barking for hours until Kalman was found by a local smallholder with a horse-drawn cart who had likewise failed to escape the storm. A little scared, the man carefully loaded Kalman's limp body and his bicycle onto the cart, leaving Toza to worriedly run alongside all the way to the village.

2.

THE SMALLHOLDER TOOK Kalman's unconscious body home and immediately informed Doctor Bariša Radičev what had happened. Doctor Radičev made haste to Kalman's house, not forgetting to also inform old Anton Klet. Anton anxiously rushed over from the other end of the village, nervously recalling his recently passed Nanny Eva, who for reasons of her own had tied him to Kalman far more than his position would otherwise require. And there he was once more, hurrying along despite the fact that he had retired from the post of Orphanage Father. And even had he not, it was highly unlikely that Kalman would still be his responsibility. In a small room, lit only by the murky light of the overcast day, Kalman lay under a blanket. At his side was Doctor Radičev. Anton stepped worriedly toward the injured man and the doctor, but stopped short when he noticed a lump in the blanket at the position of Kalman's penis. "Strange thing," said the doctor, turning Kalman's head to one side to show a small burn at the back of his skull. In all likelihood, he said, the lightning struck Kalman in the back of the head and exited through his penis, leaving it rigid. He pulled back the blanket from Kalman's body all the way to his belt, showing Anton an unusual reddish-brown pattern at the points where the electricity had "expelled" the blood vessels at various depths of the skin, like a fern or the branchlets of a thuja. "My lord, what on earth is this?" said Anton, clutching his chest. The doctor said there was no need to despair, since the patient was, after all, alive. The consequences were unpredictable and strange, and more would be known when Kalman awoke, which the doctor hoped would happen soon. He took from his bag some kind of ointment to be rubbed into the burns on the head and the genitals, "while we wait to see whether his mind has come to harm." Anton stepped back. This would not do. Back of the head, yes, but how could he... It was out of the question. The doctor opened his bag once more, removed a rubber glove and, with a quick hand, discreetly daubed both burns. He said he would send an old woman every day to take care of it until Kalman regained consciousness. Then he left. At which point Anton took a deep breath, collapsed onto the stool by the bed, and snarled, "Fuck, what a job."

The next morning, Kalman's burns were tended to by old Rezika, who was known for washing and preparing the dead for burial. Kalman was still unconscious, and Anton kept vigil at his side. Later that afternoon, Doctor Radičev stopped by once more and expressed concern at the patient's unchanged state and the possibility of dehydration. He wetted a piece of gauze and dabbed Kalman's face and lips, dripping a little water into his mouth. He gave notice that he would visit again in the evening when, if there was still no change, certain steps would have to be taken. At that juncture, as night fell, Kata Lorbach appeared at the door of Kalman's house, stealing ahead of old Rezika. There were channels of communication in the village that carried information quicker than Kalman. Had Kalman simply suffered an accident, she would not have taken such a bold step. Besides, she had made it perfectly clear to him that her interest in him had ended. An unrelenting electric erection, however, was a first-rate novelty, and, like the Theban maenads sent dancing off to Mount Cithaeron, Kata could not contain her curiosity. Old Anton had already heard the gossip about a certain connection between Kata and Kalman, and so, believing that Kata's motives were more romantic in nature than they really were, left the room in order to give them a little privacy. On his way out, he merely pointed out to her the small box on the table and said, "There's the ointment for the wounds."

Kata sat down by the bed, her eyes burning with curiosity, and quickly summoned the courage to pull the blanket from him so she could familiarize herself with the situation in greater detail. Regarding the unusual pattern on his body and the scorched, erect phallus, she thought for a moment how her curiosity was slightly cruel and unfeeling. So she stood and took the box of cream and once more sat down beside him. She gently rubbed the ointment first into the burn on the head, then moved her palm over the patterns on the torso and stopped at the penis. Then she scooped up a handful of ointment and took hold of it. Carefully at first, as a wound requires, she spread a thick layer over the whole of it. Kalman let out a moan, seemingly of satisfaction more than pain, and stirred. Startled, Kata stopped her hand at the base of the penis, though not releasing it from her gentle but firm and enveloping grip. Was it just satisfaction or was pain there too, she wondered. After a few moments she began to twist and turn her hand, avoiding—as much as she could—the burns and keeping pace with Kalman's increasingly intense and rapid breathing. As she gathered steam, his body tensed as if again infused with electricity, and Kata became so carried away that she ceased worrying about the burns and began energetically massaging the entire member with all her being. She felt a force grip her, briefly, for not more than a second, but so powerfully that for a moment her body froze, a paralysis that was followed by a split-second flash that lit up the entire room like a photographer's flashbulb. Kalman's body tensed further, offered a few breaths of relief, and ejaculated, before it collapsed completely, pulling with it into that languor and limpness the hitherto rigid penis. Flustered, Kata looked around her, stood up in disbelief, and rubbed her painful and still slightly numb right forearm with her left. She smiled, satisfied at the result of her efforts, took out a tissue, and wiped the semen from Kalman's stomach. Clutching the dirtied tissue with two fingers and wondering what to do with it, she was almost knocked to the ground by the sight of Kalman's startled eyes staring at her.

Kalman woke to the worst hangover he had ever known: a monstrous headache to which was attached a body that felt as if broken in two. His vision was so blurred that he could make out only silhouettes; there was a ringing in his ears, and lodged in his nose was a smell of dust mixed with the stench of singed hairs and burned tissue. Awakened by his orgasm, he stared

confused at Kata's corpulent silhouette as she stuffed the wet
tissue into her pocket and discreetly slipped out of the room,
closing the door behind her with a grin and ignoring Kalman's
nervous "who's that?" Anton burst in, calming the agitated
Kalman, and was quickly followed by Doctor Radičev. They
both began to inform him of the unfortunate events that had
unfolded and the accident that befell him—screaming to be
heard over the ringing that Kalman complained of in his ears—
and how very lucky he had been, given that events could have
ended far more tragically. They told him everything, fed him
and quenched his thirst, explained to him how to rub the ointment into his wounds—since Rezika certainly would not do so
anymore—and sent him off to sleep with the aid of a strong sed-
ative that the doctor discharged into his bloodstream. There
remained just enough time for Anton, like a train disappearing
into a tunnel, to wink slyly, roguishly, and remark that Kalman had awakened right at the moment he was visited by the
innkeeper. Kalman had no recollection; in that moment of collapse, he had not connected the silhouette with Kata. For some
reason he did not feel it particularly important. The next day,
he woke at dawn. The ringing in his ears had subsided, but his
sight was still fuzzy. Unlike the evening before, his thoughts
that morning were sharp and fluent. After a short period feeling his way about the house on all fours, he was visited again
by Anton and the doctor, who was satisfied and said that his
sight would clear up soon too. Out of the vanity he had nurtured with regard to his occupation as the only happiness that
had any particular resonance in these dark moments, Kalman
asked in panic when he would be able to return to work, and

who was standing in for him. They immediately allayed his fears with the assurance that he was irreplaceable, that his job was waiting for him, and for that very reason everything should be done to ensure a quick recovery. Then they helped him into the yard, where he was barked at by Toza, who had not left the bicycle's side, protecting it.

"Look, Toza's looking after your bicycle and waiting for you," said Anton, patting Kalman on the shoulder.

Overcome, Kalman felt a lump in his throat when Toza rubbed against his leg and sat on his foot. "Lord only knows what would have become of you and when you would have been found had he not barked," Anton added. "Feed him," Kalman murmured, at which Anton assured him that the dog was neither thirsty nor hungry. The visitors soon went on their way, leaving a half-blind Kalman sitting in his yard, taking in the warmth of the late-September sun. He at last found calm; the doctor had given him some kind of painkiller, which had done its work, so his thoughts had much more space in which to move. He turned over in his mind the notion that this whole thing with the lightning might not be so bad after all. Who else in Siga had survived a lightning strike? No one that he had heard of. There had been lightning victims, but they invariably went straight to the grave. He was now a rarity in Siga. Everyone would address him with respect. They would pepper him with questions, trying to hide the flood of obtrusive curiosity. And he, leaning grandiosely against the bar of the Tench, would slowly tell his story, embellishing it with elements that never actually occurred but that were so convincing and seemingly self-evident that they really could have actually happened. They would ask, was it true that his manhood had stood at attention an entire day? And he would open his arms and shrug helplessly, as if to say, "I can't help being so virile." Then he would drink. Oh, how he would drink. Rivers of rakija and beer would flow. He would become a greater attraction than that strongman from Sombor who was at the Olympics in Berlin. A man of the world, if you please, so special and important that the world would come to him; he would not have to go anywhere. Oh, if only he had a glass at hand right now to warm his heart. But how to find rakija now with eyes so cloudy? Perhaps he could if he tried. After all, if this very moment proved anything, it was that he didn't want for good luck. So he bravely got to his feet and began shuffling along the wall, his left hand out in front as reconnaissance. He made it to the door, carefully entered, and after a few loud bumps against the furniture, he finally came back out with a bottle of rakija in hand. "Who needs a glass?" he thought to himself, and took a swig from the bottle. He tottered back to the seat on the veranda and sat down, satisfied. Toza watched him with curiosity. He lay in the sun next to the discarded bicycle on the paved path between the gate and the entrance to the veranda (since everything else, as we know, had turned long ago into an overgrown thicket), occasionally moving to the veranda to cool off on its cold tiles.

The rakija slowly warmed Kalman's heart. Brightly colored thoughts filled and tickled his mind like some fast-growing, wild grape. Until the climax, after which came that other, heavy, bleary phase of drunkenness, which seeks to imitate the initial euphoria but fails, turning instead like some genetic mutation into a bleak and feigned copy of the original state. All the same, a person takes no heed and offers no resistance, since intoxication is powerful and seductive; the body sacrifices the mind for the ever-stronger sensation of comfort coursing through the veins. It was in such an ontologically dreary state that Kalman, quite unprepared, first heard the Voice. Quiet at first, like an incomprehensible mumbling somewhere behind his left ear, prompting him to turn around sharply, surprised that behind him there was no human blur of the kind in which his compromised sight had presented Klet and Doctor Radičev earlier that day. A little confused, he settled his nerves and focused on the Voice that had grown increasingly intelligible, so much so that he could now clearly make out Hungarian words tumbling out one after the other in a torrent, and became certain that some jokester was visiting him in his yard. He felt uncomfortable, but gave a sour smile and called out, "Who's there? Stop fucking around." He stood up and took a few steps in each direction, straining his eyes and ears to fathom where exactly this uninvited guest was hiding. His bleary eyes, however, could not make out anything, and the Voice sounded both distant and always in the same place: somewhere behind his left ear. He realized quickly that in his incomplete state he would not solve the problem, so he temporarily gave up and decided to wait for his sight to return in full. He returned to the stool, sat down, and continued to drink. He listened to the Voice like enemy artillery that an infantryman cannot get the better of and nourished his frustration for a better opportunity in which he would be able to act. The only thing he did try was to call out, "Toza, grab 'im!" But Toza gave him a puzzled look, turned around in a circle, and laid down once more beside the bicycle. "Some guard dog," Kalman said.

By early afternoon, Kalman was so drunk that in spite of the unsettling circumstances, he managed to fall asleep on the stool. He woke up a few hours later when the sun was already starting to set, having fidgeted in his sleep and tumbled from the stool onto the cold veranda floor. The first thing that came to his mind was not the headache, not the terrible hangover, or the bruising from the fall, but the realization that the Voice was still droning on relentlessly and that his sight had been completely restored. He hurriedly picked himself up from the ground and began agitatedly looking around. Panicking, he searched every nook and cranny of the yard and house, anywhere that could be searched, his horror growing exponentially as he neared the conclusion that there was no guest to be found. After an hour of frantic searching, he returned to his stool and spat on the veranda. He became gripped by an overwhelming horror that left no room in his head for anything else. He found himself on the cold, hard ground with the merciless Voice, paralyzed, powerless, and besieged. That short, chubby, dark-skinned young man with a round face and flat nose had turned into a pale apparition. With a trembling hand, he wiped away the beads of cold sweat from his brow, twitching like a nervous horse. "For God's sake, what is this?" he at last managed to ask himself before throwing up.

As his first line of defense, Kalman chose flight. Undeterred by his lightning experience, the burns, the pain, the excruciating hangover, and the head-to-toe horror—it was like he had forgotten it all—he took to his bicycle like Pegasus and tore down the street in the company of Toza. He stopped in front of the Tench, sluggishly and carelessly left the bicycle in the dog's care, and headed inside. In the gathering autumn dusk, the day's work was done and the Tench was packed to the rafters. The moment Kalman poked his head through the door, a hush fell. It turned out he had been right in his reverie earlier in the day, since everyone really did show great interest in him and his experience, so that after the initial silence they all excitedly clamored around him; some offered drinks and invited him to their table, some had clearly already heard about his electric erection and gestured proudly with upright forearms and tightly clenched fists, while others clapped and whistled or raised their glasses in his name. "Hero," cried some. "Legend," shouted others. Kalman passed through the din as if walking through a door, limply raising his arm in greeting. Deaf to the invitations, he headed for a secluded corner of the bar, up against the window, where he had been known to spend time before. Only back then, the position served as a lookout, affording him a good view of the tavern from which he would exchange remarks with others or venture briefly to their table before returning. But now he tucked himself away in that corner as a kind of seclusion. To isolate oneself among people is, for the unloved, often more comforting than total isolation. But it comes at a price, and many people never fail to interpret such behavior as directed against them, and the acute (or chronic) lack of any need for communication as contempt for them personally, since why else would someone sit in their vicinity and behave as if they are not there? And there we are—such a bizarre need had driven Kalman to place himself among other people. Some, therefore, took offense, but a few more well-meaning simply sent Kalman drinks and left him in peace. After the last drunk guest had accepted that Kalman was not in the mood and that there'd be no antics after all, normal service resumed. On the bar in front of Kalman stood several glasses of rakija that the well intentioned had sent him, an uninterrupted flow that he welcomed since he had never needed them more. Every now and again the rakija would dry up, and so Kalman would order another himself, or the innkeeper Öcsike would, unprompted, pour him more, sometimes on the house, considering it, in the manner of a good landlord, a form of investment.

Kalman hoped that the hubbub of the tavern would go some way to drowning out the Voice that had been tormenting him since the morning. He had been listening attentively, nervously, since entering, but already during the howls that met his arrival he had concluded with despair that the Voice had a special quality that made it stand out uncommonly distinct from all others. What a defeat. Hence why he again concluded that the smartest course of action was to surrender to the influence of the alcohol in the hope that something would change. Perhaps, if he could get through the day, the Voice would disappear of its own accord. That's when he started to quietly reflect, after the rakija had nicely anesthetized him and freed him to string together a few thoughts. The Voice was still babbling away, but his booze-soaked brain finally gave little heed. With sunken shoulders, all meager and penitent, Kalman sat at the bar like a defendant in court. At some point last call was announced, with Kalman by then laid out in a corner, but he refused to respond when Öcsike tried to wake him and get him to leave, since the idea of returning home in the dead of night filled him with even greater horror. However, not only did Öcsike's efforts in unnecessarily wake him from the slumber he had worked so hard to reach, but, after Öcsike had left the Tench at around two in the morning and locked the door behind him, Kalman lurched to his feet to sort himself out with a few deciliters of mulberry rakija to return him to a state of such terrible intoxication that he was reduced to crawling. Yet at the moment he passed out, his face was lit up with relief, as if he had been blessed.

Öcsike woke him at about six with a gentle kick; outside, the sun was coming up. Kalman had pissed himself, and so Öcsike made him quickly scrub the bit of floor he had dirtied. He complied, asked for another drink, knocked it back, and just as quickly sat on his bicycle and hurried off, fleeing the despair that followed close behind. Toza, of course, hurried after him. At home, as he changed his trousers, stumbling and cursing, tears began to flow. That can happen sometimes, he thought, blaming his inebriation. But he sensed that these tears were different. He did not stay long at home, not so much out of fear (for some reason it felt easier during daytime) as the need to be constantly in flight. So he jumped on his bicycle as soon as he had changed and set off in the direction of the Village Hall, accompanied by the inseparable Toza. Somewhere along the way he met old Anton Klet, who was visibly upset since he and Doctor Radičev had visited Kalman the night before, but he was nowhere to be found. Disappointed and not a little angry, the doctor had gone home. Anton suspected where Kalman might have been; so be it, he thought, it's up to him whether he'll lie in bed or not, but let it be known that rakija never helped anyone. "Oh, Nanny Eva, how have I wronged you, my God?" Anton cried,

IVAN VIDAK

then waved him away angrily and continued down the street all flushed with agitation, calling out only to tell Kalman that he must see the doctor as soon as possible, as a matter of urgency. Little of that got through to Kalman. Only in the agony of self-preservation did it strike him that it really would be good to visit the doctor, since he might be the only one able to help. A moment later he was in the Village Hall and, to everyone's surprise, asking for the day's news and his drum. The municipal officials regarded him as they would some natural wonder, and paid special attention to the burn on his head. How, why, they marveled. Shouldn't he be in bed? Taking the news and the drum, Kalman shook them off like a swarm of annoying flies, displaying a dramatic lack of patience. He quickly remounted his bicycle and in no time at all was at the first crossroads. Clenching his teeth, he thumped away at the drum harder than ever:

Hear ye, hear ye!

Italy, Germany, and Japan seal military alliance in Berlin!

District committee for protection against aerial attack issues pamphlet entitled "Instructions for Protection from Aerial Attack on Siga Municipality"!

Thirty-two persons attend annual assembly of the House of Young Artisans. Joining the board are: Ivan Kromer, Đerđ Urbanovski, Antun Plavšin, Ivan Rang, and Ivan Burghart!

Notified!

To holler brought him relief. Slight and fleeting, like a shiver, but nonetheless relief. And then he realized he had omitted the kind of quip he usually signed off with. He stopped, stuttered, like he had tripped on a stone or was tied to a leash but really wanted to go on. The whole thing ended in an angry, frustrated drumbeat, followed by incoherent yelling and a short final cry of powerlessness: "Bollocks!" It was one of those rare moments when a few heads peered through windows or gates to hear what "that man" was shouting about. All that remained was to visit the other eleven crossroads, which he did, bursting with motivation and an unprecedented appetite, before hurrying off to see the doctor.

Suddenly he feared the doctor, since he knew him to possess a host of questions and a penetrating gaze, both of which at this moment seemed like the perfect means to exhaust and undermine what little strength was holding him together. How to tell the doctor that he was hearing a Voice of unknown provenance, but which happened to know everything about him and had no qualms about saying the most monstrous things to him? How, when he knew not what to tell himself nor was in any state to accept that he was hearing anything at all? What until just a moment before had seemed like a possible solution now weighed him down. So he took some heart when he walked in on Doctor Radičev, a tall, mustachioed man on the cusp of his forties, in military uniform. A packed bag sat on the veranda, while the doctor meticulously shaved his face in a small mirror on the wall. On a stool next to him sat a large, elderly gentleman with a long gray beard and hair and small, lively eyes. Poor Doctor Radičev, you see, had been called up for military exercises from which he would never return. It turned out that the elderly gentleman next to him was a retired doctor who had once served in Lemeš and was now about to stand in for Radičev. Catching sight of Kalman's bloodshot, inflamed eyes and his generally tortured physical appearance, Radičev broke off shaving and began reprimanding him. Is he crazy? Does he grasp at all the seriousness of his state? Who knows what may have become of him after leaving his bed so suddenly! And straight away he sat Kalman on the stool on which until that point had been sitting the aged doctor, Aleksandar Penić, who was now, so as not to get in the way, playing with Toza. Under the circumstances, every additional voice was too much for Kalman. His face was gripped with nervousness and all kinds of fresh tics, his unsettled gaze wandering like that of a lonely tracker. For even though he constantly heard the Voice, Kalman imagined eyes all around him, his ákousma pressing in on him like a thousand hidden and inquisitive looks. Having berated and then checked him, Doctor Radičev gave a sigh of relief and concluded that his general state was satisfactory, but nevertheless firmly advised that he spend some more time in bed. And, in the strongest terms possible, he warned him off drink. There was no reply from Kalman, other than a few glances and facial spasms, and then he turned toward his bicycle, which Radičev took as an opportunity to introduce him to Doctor Penić and so kept him in the yard. Doctor Penić at first glance appeared a very calm and pleasant man. He confessed to Kalman that he found his case exceptionally interesting and that he had once before encountered a similar example of a man surviving a lightning strike. This stopped Kalman in his tracks, and he swung around toward Doctor Penić. Is it possible, he hoped. Immediately Kalman flooded the older man with questions that poured out with such force that both doctors were left astonished by the sudden change in him. The questions tumbled out one on top of the other, and all of them in one way or another concerned the experience of the "human lightning rod" Penić had encountered. "Easy, my friend," Doctor Penić said with a smile, giving him a friendly pat on the shoulder. He invited Kalman to his home that evening to talk over a drink. Kalman knew enough to hold back from further questioning (although he wanted with all his heart to keep going), said goodbye, and rode off on his bicycle.

Kalman, trembling, wondered how to spend the day, though his course had been mapped out some time ago: the shortest route to the Tench. The good news he'd heard from Penić, although still little more than a flicker of hope, gave his being the push and the strength it needed to withstand, to a degree, the all-permeating terror of the Voice, or at least cope with it a little more easily. The Tench was practically empty. Besides two workers talking quietly in a corner, there was only Öcsike. Kalman was in no state to consume that midday calm, so he knocked back a few rakijas and set off on his afternoon round hours ahead of schedule. Since Kalman of late hardly ever remembered to feed him, Toza hoped that Öcsike would once more fill his stomach. That didn't happen, so he complained unhappily before chasing after the bicycle, only to recall, when it was already too late, a bone he had left by a bush. The drumming and yelling at twelve village crossroads once again brought Kalman short-lived relief, but only for as long as it took him to finish, not a moment more. What now? Getting blind drunk was out of the question, since he couldn't turn up like that at the doctor's, nor would it make any sense seeking answers half-conscious. But the time had to be passed. Given that at that moment, because of the Voice, he did not have the mental capacity to come up with anything else, he continued riding his bike, visiting various corners of Siga and beating out the news in places he was never expected to. That's how they heard him for the first, and last, time in the Gypsy quarter on the edge of Siga, where in no time at all the curious folk had gathered around him, creating the kind of audience he had rarely seen; in front of the boatyard, where the workers were particularly put out, believing that the authorities wanted to inform them about some kind of emergency, something they were sure not to like; then in front of the inns and taverns, including the Tench, drinking a rakija at each—only one, not to overdo it; outside shops, businesses... He caused a veritable storm among the masses; almost everyone thought war was being announced or some other kind of disaster. In the end he ran over into the regular evening round of the usual twelve crossroads like a rondeau returning to where it started.

It was very nearly dark when he stepped into the yard of the doctor's house, left his bicycle, and turned toward the doors through which shone the light of a kerosene lamp. When night fell, Siga became eerily dark. The light of a candle or lamp would sometimes sneak miserly through a window, in small doses, hardly enough for a person to find their way and not wander off God knows where in the complete darkness—the kind of darkness that with the advent of electricity people all but forgot and which survived, with all its metaphysical weight and natural purpose, only in stories of old. Only in the center of the village were there a few nonelectric streetlights. Though Kalman was perhaps unaware, his profession was already becoming its own kind of atavism. In the months when dusk would descend early, town drummers who lit their way with a lamp, wading through the dark bearing news like some eerie torchbearer, were increasingly rare. In Siga, however, such times were still to come, and now, as he looked at the dimly lit windows of the doctor's home, Kalman shuddered with unease and the chill of the autumn air. He knocked on the door. "Come!" thundered old Penić, who coughed to clear his throat. The interior seemed bare. The outgoing doctor had clearly packed assiduously, while Doctor Penić's suitcases lay open and still full in the middle of the room. The doctor had been reading when Kalman walked in, and, getting up from the bed, he began fixing his shirt and his tousled hair.

"Come in, my dear fellow, please. Sit down, make yourself comfortable." The doctor smiled warmly, gesturing to a chair by the wall. In the time it took Kalman to nervously park his backside, the doctor had already poured two glasses of rakija and offered one to Kalman. He gratefully accepted and watched as Doctor Penić hurriedly rifled through his suitcase in search of something. He quickly approached Kalman, holding a black leather doctor's bag in one hand and in the other the bottle of rakija, from which he immediately topped up his guest's glass. Examining the burn on his head, he muttered, "This is good, yes. I wouldn't bandage that...let it breathe... But it needs cream." He took from his bag a new kind of ointment, foul smelling and almost black, rubbed it into Kalman's head, and offered him the rest of the monstrous paste. "Rub that into it; forget the stuff my colleague gave you," he added. Then he took a step back and said, "Now let's see the other problem." Embarrassed, Kalman hesitated. "Come on, come on!" said the doctor. "You think I like it? But we have to. How otherwise?" After the patient had dejectedly dropped his trousers, Doctor Penić, without approaching, glanced cursorily over his genitals. The same conclusion: cream. After telling him he could get dressed, the doctor remarked, as if in passing, that he should wash it more often, and grimaced. Because of infections, he added. But Kalman was so flooded with shame that he simply registered the information and sat down on the chair, jaded by the humiliation he was being subjected to. Prompted by Doctor Penić, Kalman told him the chronology of what had happened, what he remembered, and what others (primarily Anton) had told him—everything, except about the Voice that flogged him relentlessly.

"Interesting," said the doctor.

Stammering, Kalman reminded the doctor about the experience he had previously mentioned with the lightning-strike survivor. Hastily, in a few short sentences, the doctor told Kalman how in the months after the electric incident, the unfortunate individual from Lemeš had become inexplicably aggressive. He was capable of attacking anyone at any moment, so they quickly locked him up in a shed, being a threat to others. Someone shot him one night, out of pity. No one ever found out who did it, but more interestingly, no one ever really asked. That is, people certainly wondered, but no one ever tried to solve that riddle, and the whole case, at least for most people, was quickly closed. The lightning bolt struck the unfortunate wretch—Stipica was his name—in the shoulder and came out through the palm of the same arm. Nothing overly dramatic in terms of aftereffects, except psychological, of course.

Doctor Penić poured them each another glass of rakija, sat down opposite Kalman, and went on to explain how Stipica, besides the lightning strike, had a fairly unhinged family history, chock-full of oddballs. So it remained unclear what role his unexpected electrification had in his madness. Perhaps it set off something latent, who knows? Though he had hoped things might unfold differently and that he might be able to share with Doctor Penić his acoustic troubles, Kalman was now resigned to defeat. He figured that tonight all he might get from the doctor was a drinking chum. What else, when he clearly knew nothing about the Voice? They kept drinking. The doctor talked more and more, carried away on a wave of intoxication, while Kalman listened and drank frantically, trying to subdue the adrenaline and anxiety, to numb his being entirely. One glass followed another, and Doctor Penić soon started speaking about his travels, mainly around Germany. He told Kalman all about the wonders of phrenology—even measuring his skull—and about race theories, the new spirit of Germany, and superiority, and then about Croatianhood and the Croatian suffering within the Kingdom of Yugoslavia. Kalman paid little attention, listening to his stories as if to an uninspiring sermon. Nevertheless, he sometimes forced a smile or interrupted with the odd question. Through all that alcohol and those words, Doctor Penić seemed less and less like a figure of authority armed with knowledge, and increasingly Kalman saw the human in him: the poor moral foundations and the odor of an overweight body. And then the drunken doctor got to the story that completely sobered up Kalman and set his heart racing.

Sometime in the early twenties, on a visit to Munich, he attended a lecture on die Sprechmaschine, a kind of speaking machine devised by Wolfgang von Kempelen that was exhibited at the time in Munich's Deutsches Museum. The machine consisted of a wooden box with a bellows at one end that played the role of the lungs, and at the other a rubber funnel as the mouth, which had to be manipulated by hand while the machine, as it were, spoke. Inside the box were all sorts of valves that also had to be operated, but if one was to become adept, the results could be frightening. "My friend, you would not believe the strange feeling we were all seized by when we first heard a human voice and human words that, in all likelihood, did not come from a human mouth. We looked at each other in silence and consternation and shuddered with horror," said the doctor. The lecture, in fact, had been an overture to the first encounter with broadcast radio that around the same time, still in its infancy, was getting underway in Germany. Penić blathered on enthusiastically about the miracles of the modern world, the monstrous voices coming out of all sorts of boxes, about electricity, and the mysticism of knowledge. And then Kalman saw his chance. All of a sudden he came to see Doctor Penić as a friend in need, a fellow sufferer, practically a comrade in arms—as if fate itself had brought them together!

"I hear a Voice. He speaks only Hungarian, but I think he understands any language. He says he's my father, but I never met my father. He doesn't hear my thoughts, but he knows everything about me," Kalman announced, silencing the doctor instantaneously. The doctor was left shocked, more by the intensity of Kalman's excitement than by his words. "Since the lightning," he continued, and confessed everything in a torrent of words that Doctor Penić to a degree experienced as an imitation of that noise that Kalman was hearing and describing.

He listened carefully, not saying a word, and then in the end, showing little apparent interest, stood up, stretched, and told Kalman nonchalantly, "These things can be difficult." Then he opened the door with the words "you'll forgive me, but it's already very late, I'm tired," and, simulating a smile, joked how he was, after all, old, and tiredness comes with age. Taken aback, Kalman stood up and made his way, humiliated, to the door, through which he was dispatched with a cold "goodbye." He stepped out into the night completely confused, but above all disappointed, and struggled to understand how the doctor had heard him out and tossed him into the street like a run-of-the-mill lunatic.

Without much thought, he resolved to finally go home. He felt something inside him changing, but he couldn't make out what. The moment he entered the house and closed the door behind him, he was almost suffocated by a feeling of powerlessness and sadness. Even the Voice faded for a time. Kalman pitied himself, while simultaneously searching for a candle to light the house. He eventually found one, but then the matches presented an even bigger problem. He looked in all the usual places—the windowsill, the table, next to the oven—but the box of matches was nowhere to be found. And when he had decided to toss that torment on the warm embers of self-pity, he heard the rustling of matches in a dark corner where his late grandmother's loom stood. Before he could even be properly frightened—and could anything ever really frighten him with such force, since the appearance of the Voice?—there flew toward him from the shadows a dark and corpulent figure. The first thing he discerned was that it was a woman, though certainly not Kata Lorbach, since it was not her smell. This one smelled of sour goat's milk and was incongruously large, much older, and had monstrous breasts that immediately pinned him to the floor. However much he resisted, her weight was simply too great for a short man unaccustomed to physical work. As he struggled, Kalman felt how she took him, gasping passionately, by his injured member, which simultaneously betrayed him and began to grow in her hands. Before he knew it she had begun riding him, giving him yet another lesson in the agony of satisfaction and losing herself until a brief flash that lit up the room. At the same time, something shook her wildly, like an electric shock. Then came the predictable descent into bodily oblivion. "It's true," she whispered in his ear, still shaking. She stole through the darkness, tossing on his stomach the rustling box of matches. Pain and satisfaction spread from Kalman's groin, his spine, and his brain, through his entire body, permeating and camouflaging one another. He felt shame in himself and, even worse, in the unseen eyes of the Voice, though he felt somewhat hidden behind the veil of darkness, or was it the exhaustion that convinced him of this? He finally fell asleep, as if hidden in some deep hole, while the Voice thundered and flared in the night sky above him.

* * *

Kalman spent the next few months in a state of stupor. Such apathy brought relief, but something was stampeding somewhere beneath the surface, and Kalman sensed his relief would not last forever. He continued beating the drum and drinking, but only grudgingly, without any real motivation, to save himself and give the day meaning, so that time would not become amorphous, since when it is, it seems to last even longer. And that would not do. Sometimes, in the dark, unknown women would wait for him, help themselves to him and gratefully bid farewell, while he would surrender, prostrate, waiting not for sweet satisfaction to course through his veins but shame and humiliation, since he felt nothing else before the unseen eyes of the Voice. It was as if he hoped that the shame would be less if the act brought no concrete happiness. Only then did he notice an interesting thing: with each bolt of spurting semen, for a split second the woman on top of him would light up and shake. Only then, when his helplessness had brought him calm, did he really register it. It was so brief that one might have taken it for a trick of the light on a blinking eye. But there was no doubt: the women would be struck by something brief and powerful, to which Kalman felt no kind of direct connection.

Sometime before Christmas 1940, unsure why or what he was hoping for, Kalman resolved to visit Kata Lorbach on Christmas Eve. Kalman had never committed to memory the words Anton had whispered to him as he sank into sleep that night: she had visited him while he was freshly recovering. All it was, in fact, was a quest for some semblance of comfort or sanctuary. No sooner had he entered the inn and met her gaze than two youngish Nazis threw him out and closed the solid wood double doors. He tried to intercept her early the next morning too as she returned from church, appearing suddenly at her side as she opened the door. Not saying a word, he looked at her imploringly, to which she calmly brushed his hand from her arm and said quietly, "I have a pistol inside; don't come here anymore." She stepped away. Coincidentally or not, that night he really could have died. But fate had other plans. Around dawn on Saint Stephen's Day, the day after Christmas, Kalman was found half-frozen by the old Gypsy Đura Lulaš. Đura lived with his family tucked away in the forest, and that morning they were on their way to church for the first morning Mass. First they happened upon a barking Toza and the bicycle next to frost-covered scrub some ten meters from the road that runs from Siga to the riverbank at the Tench. Đura stopped his wagon and walked to the spot, where he then found Kalman. He woke when Đura shook him, but was so frozen through that he could hardly move. Đura picked him up and carried him to the wagon, returning for the bicycle. They wrapped him in a blanket that they had been using to fend off the cold, and Đura's wife, at his instruction, squeezed up close to Kalman and embraced him. Never had he felt anything so tender as her warm breath on his cheek. He smiled at the two girls, who watched him with curiosity.

"What is it, Kalman?" Đura asked him warmly. "You're always drunk. What's troubling you?"

With difficulty, but without hesitation, as if finally among friends and people he could trust, Kalman replied, "The Voice."

"What voice?" Đura replied.

"The voice of my father speaks to me, tells me all sorts, terrible things."

"But where is your father?" Đura asked, surprised.

"I don't know. In America, I guess. If he's alive. I've never seen him."

Đura paused to think, topped up his pipe, and lit it. As he thought, he puffed out small clouds of sweet-smelling smoke that blended in the cold air with the mist from his mouth. A good five minutes passed before he uttered, "And what does that father of yours want?"

"I don't know, haven't asked," replied Kalman.

"Ask him, don't be afraid," said Đura, tapping out his pipe on the iron-bound rim of the wagon.

They wanted to take him to the doctor, but Kalman resisted, as much as he was able, and begged them to carry him home. There they wrapped him in eiderdown, lit the fire in the stove, and did all they could to make him comfortable. Kalman continued trying to convince them that he did not need a doctor and that he would be fine as soon as he warmed up. And he implored them not to say anything to old Anton Klet if they were to meet him in church; he's old, there's no sense in worrying him unnecessarily. Warmly, if belatedly, they wished him Happy Christmas and left. A few hours later they brought him some food that the priest and sisters had sent. They could have sworn that Kalman was locked in lively conversation with someone. Entering, they found him completely alone but in surprisingly good spirits. Veritably festive.

3.

ANTON KLET DIED in January 1941. From straining on the toilet, they said. All day they hacked at the frozen ground with axes and picks to dig the grave. The circle of people in black, set against the shining, white, snow-covered expanse of the cemetery, was pretty big, understandably so, given the amount of goodness that lean and worried old man had shared out. Only Kalman stood a little apart, in thought. He remembered everything well. How could he not, having lasted the longest as one of Anton's orphans? The old man had taken care of him more than Kalman took care of himself. It went a lot further than the ambitions of Nanny Eva. Only a few months later would Kalman come to understand how far that care went, when in a moment of trouble he recalled how, a few years earlier, Anton had spared him from recruitment, with the help of the village warden at the time and the rest of the village authorities, and later, as a consequence, mobilization.

"I know he's not my father," Kalman muttered to the Voice in Hungarian, walking toward the cemetery exit. He moved separately from the crowd, behind everyone else. Most headed to The Duck, where the village authorities had organized a wake. When Kalman did not stop at the inn but kept shuffling along the frozen road, the warden's coachman, Milko, called out to him, "Come for a drink, Kalman!" Kalman waved him away and continued down the road. He stopped at the Village Hall to pick up his drum and to visit Toza, who was now stationed there, since that was where the bicycle spent the winter. Kalman had plenty of room for him in his yard, but that wouldn't have been the best solution. Though he had not quite admitted it to himself, this was far simpler for him. He was in no state to look after an animal. Besides, in his yard Toza would for the most part have been alone, but here in the Village Hall, with those in charge, there was always someone, always something. Nor would he go hungry. Kalman stopped by often, just as he had then, to collect his drum and the news and set off for the first crossroads.

Hear ye, hear ye!
  The English bomb Napoli!
  Fighting continues in North Africa!
  Josip Kovač is the new president of Danube football club. Forty members attend the assembly. Mata Šimunov becomes secretary, Mata Horvat treasurer, and Stipan Šuvak, Mata Pašić, and Marin Vinkov are picked for the board!
  Anton Klet was buried today. The service is tomorrow at six!
  Notified!

IVAN VIDAK

He had completely given up on those humorous afterthoughts. No doubt, Kalman seemed changed. For a start, he no longer drank. No one noticed at first. In truth, no one cared whether he drank or not, except perhaps for the people from the Village Hall, for whom he became a bit easier to deal with. At the end of the day, almost everyone in Siga drank, some more, some less. It was practically proof of manhood. But among the village gossips, there was something new: some had heard him talking to himself. This attracted greater attention to him, which in turn led people to notice that he was not drinking. And when the hearsay was confirmed, nothing could dislodge the opinion that the mask had finally fallen from what was nothing more than an ordinary village idiot. Some claimed it was wrong to expect anything else of him; others blamed the drink, and more still poked fun at him, playing telephone and guessing at what Kalman might have been muttering in Hungarian. They swore that it was like he was talking to someone. But, as these things go, the novelty soon wore off, and Kalman was left alone. They finally accepted this oddity as his own affair, particularly since this symptom of madness posed no particular threat to anyone, and Kalman was still capable of doing his job.

Kalman had, therefore, entered into a relationship with the Voice. Since that morning when Lulaš had saved him from the cold, things had started to change significantly. For the first few weeks he left the house only for work, three times a day, spending the rest of the time indoors. Then, leaving the house with the words "Got it, Dad, I understand now," he would visit boatyards, artisans, day workers—almost anyone with a job— and ask about affairs and relations at work. He would also ask whether they had heard of communism. "War is coming," he would say conspiratorially as he left, raising a forefinger to his closed lips. People looked at him confused, like he was indeed the very madman he had been spoken of. And these were the somewhat bizarre activities Kalman was engaged in when March 27 arrived. It was on that day a putsch in Belgrade overthrew the Yugoslav government, two days after it had signed the Vienna Protocol on Yugoslav accession to the Berlin Pact, igniting protests, "Better War Than a Pact, Better the Grave Than a Slave," and everything else that went on until March 30, when the schoolchildren were sent home and it became clear that something serious was afoot. "Joke all you like, that Kalman isn't as mad as you think," Mika Tišljer said on April 7, watching Kalman ride off, having delivered the news that morning about the first German bombing of Belgrade and the attack on the Kingdom of Yugoslavia the day before. Interestingly, from that moment on every one of Kalman's twelve crossroads had its own regular audience: loyal, passionate, and curious. They would frequently stop him, call after him, and seek additional explanation of his often skeletal news items, which otherwise served to provoke more than to inform. But Kalman was professional and unyielding.

In the Sombor sector and its surroundings, there had been no military contact with the Hungarian army (it was the Hungarians, not the Germans, who attacked Bačka). The Yugoslav army got the order to abandon its military positions on April 12, which it did while bringing down bridges behind it: toward Lugomir and the Vinograd bridge toward the village. The same day, the Hungarian Honvéd army entered Bačka, and with it

Siga. For many residents of Siga, this came as a great surprise. Even many Hungarians were caught out by the arrival of the Hungarian army, which they had not expected, and it came as a particular surprise to the Germans at Kata Lorbach's inn, the men of the Kulturbund. They had expected the mighty Wehrmacht and instead got the Hungarians, and for many of them this was a huge disappointment. Over the days that followed, two hundred people of various nationalities in the Sombor region were killed and thousands were arrested, among them many from Siga.

So on April 12, the Honvéd entered Siga. They hastily put in place a new authority, left four police officers, and assigned four guards to the Village Hall before pulling back to Sombor, where they were stationed. Mihály Andrássy, a farmer, became the new—and, under the new nomenklatura, the first—mayor of Siga. He would remain in the post right up until October 21, 1944. Alongside Mihály, Béla Hámori-Hauke was appointed clerk, and the two of them constituted the axis of power in Siga.

That same evening, April 12, Kalman was called to a meeting at the Village Hall. For him the day had been particularly confusing, since not only for the first time was the news not waiting for him at the Village Hall, but the hall itself was completely abandoned. He arrived by bicycle, greeted the newly appointed guards at the entrance—all of them familiar Siga Hungarians—and stepped inside nervously. There he walked in on Mihály in the midst of appointing Ferenc Kovács as head teacher of the school and organizing lessons with him. In Hungarian, Croatian, and German. No Serbian. With them was Mrs. Ildiko Loparić, for years the Hungarian language teacher. Kalman entered and greeted them with a sheepish "zdravo," to which Mrs. Loparić angrily turned round and let it be known in Hungarian that Šokac dialect should not be spoken, that everyone has to be Hungarian since this was Hungarian land. Confused, Kalman stopped, but fortunately Mihály intervened, welcomed him warmly, and informed Loparić and Ferenc that they would continue later. He invited Kalman to sit down, walked the teacher and headteacher to the door, summoned the clerk, Béla, and sat down with him in front of Kalman. Smiling smugly, they offered him palinka and began to tell him what an important historical moment this was for the Hungarian people, that they knew who his father was (a communist, but nevertheless one of ours, a Hungarian!), that they were aware of his considerable care for his roots, that he later even learned Hungarian, and how it would be good if he were to join with the new authorities and serve his homeland in the way he knew best: as town drummer. Nothing meaningful would change, they said, "except that we are now masters of our own land, as they say." So for Kalman, continuing his service could only be better than it was "under the Serbs." Kalman refused the palinka but readily nodded his head. "Persze"—"of course"—he said in the Hungarian they were naturally now speaking. This delighted Mihály and clerk Béla. They leapt up, embraced Kalman, and arm in arm the three of them went out into the yard to share the happy news with the guards. All-Hungarian euphoria broke out. A little over-the-top perhaps, but that's what happens when yokels band together and begin to seek legitimacy and some symbol of continuity. In this case, Kalman, well-known to everyone, was the perfect fit. One of the guards even shot into the air and let fly a completely

IVAN VIDAK

pointless profanity. Mihály quickly stopped him, but, all the same, the outburst heralded the end of their little celebration. They told Kalman that they expected him the next morning, to pick up his drum and the news. "I'll listen, Dad, if you say that's the best way," Kalman later told the Voice, parking the bicycle and Toza inside the gate of his house.

The next morning, he encountered an unusual commotion at the Village Hall. It turned out that at some point in the last few nights, Doctor Aleksandar Penić, completely unimpeded and obviously with the help of at least one accomplice, had defaced and robbed a grave at the Jewish cemetery, located near the boatyard right outside Siga. Early that morning, he crossed the Danube at Bezdan and probably continued through Baranja into the mists of the Independent State of Croatia. In all likelihood he met his end there, since he was never heard from again. The majority of Jews had left Siga a decade earlier during the Great Depression, most of them moving to Sombor as a larger economic center. The old synagogue at number fifty-five Church Street was left to fall into disrepair in the yard of a private house, and now served as the police headquarters. That is, the new authority posted four Hungarian officers there as insurance. One should not confuse them with the four guards of the Village Hall, who were appointed from the ranks of local Hungarians; the police were Hungarians from Hungary, who had not an ounce of sentimentality or understanding for the local population and its circumstances.

Hence how that turbulent morning in the Village Hall, when the officers were unenthusiastically compiling a report about the defacement of the grave, they decided to commandeer

Kalman's bicycle. Because they liked it. After all, why should they be constantly walking, having to negotiate the muddy streets? If their superiors had not even deigned to leave them some kind of vehicle, a bicycle would do fine. Kalman was still weighing up his vengefulness and the humiliation that the Doctor Penić incident had subjected him to, when all of a sudden, one of the officers approached the bicycle, sat on it, and rode off between his colleagues, triggering a salvo of approval and delight. They immediately dropped their tedious work on the Jewish cemetery and happily went out into the street, where the one who had the idea of taking the bicycle taught the others how to ride it. In fright, Kalman went out after them, his eyes shifting between the bicycle and Toza, who was merrily running around among them, trying to make it known that he had no intention of being separated from the bicycle, not for all the bones in the world. The officers quickly accepted him, laughing at his antics and even christening him Csángó, after a Hungarian ethnic group that lived in Romania. Kalman looked on sadly and, not knowing the name of his bicycle, uttered a muffled "Toza." Mihály and clerk Béla quickly appeared at his side in front of the gate of the Village Hall, along with two guards from the morning shift. They recognized the injustice, but were convinced that, for the greater good, that was how it would have to be. Those are our boys, Kalman, our officers, they said. They probably need the bicycle more than you. Kalman turned toward the two armed guards with a look that asked, "Aren't you going to do anything?" With another look, Mihály ordered them back into the yard, patted Kalman on the shoulder, and told him that our boys would take care of the bicycle

IVAN VIDAK

and Toza. Then he left Kalman to watch how the merry band of Hungarian police officers carried off down the street at least half of everything he had. "Am I a Jew too?" Kalman disappointedly asked the Voice. He stared down the street until they had disappeared around the corner.

From New Year, more precisely from Christmas, Kalman had a drive about him, a focus. He really did. How else to describe such a great change? In the space of a few months, for example, he had completely altered his routine. Not once had he been in the Tench. He began frequenting other places, more civilized places, more popular, more orderly. Sometimes he would tell the Voice, "That's not for me," but would obviously run into a paternal resistance that, regardless of his sour grimaces, his angry snorts, and the bitter lump in his throat, would always know how to bend him to his will. The Duck was the focal point of the village notables. There, no one paid much attention to your nationality or faith. Everyone was the same if they were important, and Kalman, given his post as town drummer, was at least formally on the cusp of such a status. Among the people who stopped by were those in charge of Siga, the odd wealthy trader, the undertaker, the priest, not to mention the doctor when he was in Siga (the serious landowners did not mix with them; they were a world unto themselves). Kalman would sit among these civic leaders, drink milk, and eat the strudel that old Evča Patkova would bake and sell at the bar. There were more substantial offerings on the menu too, from the stove and from the oven, depending on the day, and many bachelors had their meals there. It was the closest thing Siga had to a restaurant. It also hosted a range of balls throughout the year: the hunters' ball, beekeepers, firemen, fancy dress... Then The Duck would become unusually lively. Besides changing his regular inn, Kalman also began getting his house and yard in order. Within a few days he managed to root out the forest that had taken over and in which he had once found such satisfaction and peace. All of it was cleared and the ground turned over and raked, ready for the crop seeds that Kalman had been agonizing over. Besides that, he replaced loose nails, tightened screws, changed one long-broken window pane, and leveled out the earthen floor, giving it a fresh coat of lime. "How do I do this?" he would ask the Voice in the tone of a puzzled child faced with a challenge. Then, by trial and error, nervously at first but later with more and more patience, he would come up with a solution and a satisfactory result. He even made a kennel for Toza and placed it by the gate, on the inside, right there where he had always left his bicycle. The effort rubbed salt into the wound inflicted by the police, but the purpose was to give form to his hope.

Kalman was more than a little surprised when one day in late July, the Voice ordered him back to the Tench. "You're fucking kidding me," Kalman replied, courageously if a little uncertainly, but he nevertheless pulled on his rucksack and set off on a long, roundabout route through the forest to cover his tracks. He arrived at the Tench a little after midday. The tavern was practically empty: besides Öcsike, the only other people there were Stipan Tucakov, Adam Štrangar, and Nikola-Mika Šimunov, all sitting at the same table. Öcsike was pleased to see him and slapped him on the back. But the other three scowled at him and somehow drew closer to one another, dropping their heads and continuing their conversation. Innkeeper Öcsike clearly knew what was going on, as if he were keeping watch over the situation, so he called over to Kalman when he saw him trying to settle in next to the trio, all worked up and frightened as if someone was forcing him.

"Kalman, what d'you want over there? Come here, your old spot—I've been saving it for you!" Öcsike called.

Unwilling but also evidently relieved, Kalman heeded him and took his seat at the bar.

"So what do you do, now you don't drink?" Öcsike asked him, completely genuinely.

Kalman had no ready answer, shrugged, ears alert, and replied, "I scratch my balls. Forget it…"

Öcsike gave a delighted snigger, handed him the glass of water he asked for, and walked out with a broom.

"Dad, how do you understand everything, but you only speak Hungarian?" Kalman asked the Voice a little rebelliously, which, judging by the grimace he made, he probably quickly regretted. The three troublemakers at the table cast him the occasional cold and distrustful look, but did not halt their conversation. "What? Dad, you must be crazy. They'll kill me!" Kalman said to the Voice, and started sweating as if he had a fever, even trembling in panic. "Translate it for them? Surely I'm not going to do it in Hungarian?" he said. Finally he gathered himself, approached the men, and began drumming furiously on top of the next table, at the same rhythm at which he would beat the drum, and began yelling:

"Peoples of Yugoslavia—Serbs, Croats, Slovenes, Montenegrins, Macedonians, and others! You are defeated in war, but subjugated you are not. Your grandfathers' glorious tradition of justice and freedom must not be forgotten. Now is the time to show you are worthy descendants. Now is the time, the moment has come for you to rise up as one in the fight against the occupiers and those who serve them, the oppressors of our peoples."

Tucakov, Štrangar, and Šimunov stood up from the table as if on fire. They looked at each other briefly in panic before Tucakov pulled a knife from his sock and stepped forward. "Grab him! We've no choice." They threw themselves on Kalman, and in no time at all they wrestled him to the floor, Stipan Tucakov holding the blade to his throat.

"I'm on your side! I'm on your side, I swear," Kalman cried, the color draining from his face.

Encouraged by having overcome the suspect, Tucakov asked him how he could be on their side when he was Hungarian. Kalman quickly pointed out that the innkeeper Öcsike was also Hungarian, but was there nevertheless. That gave them pause for thought, calmed them even, but they pressed on with the interrogation regardless.

"Öcsike is one of ours, it's true, but Öcsike didn't cozy up straight away with the occupiers, unlike you."

"People, I'm on your side, I tell you. Whose side could I be on? I've been plotting from the inside from the very first day, I swear! My father was Hungarian, true, but he was a communist and a friend of our peoples who saved him when he needed it most. And I'm not only Hungarian. At the end of the day, aren't we all brothers in communism?"

"Prove it!" they replied.

How can I prove that to you here, he thought, what would win you over? Kalman swore that he knew all there was to know about communism, just ask. And the three whispered conspiratorially among themselves, exchanged glances, and concluded that a spy would know that too. That's it, Kalman realized, let them use him as their spy, that's how he would prove it. They paused once more, contemplated, whispered. They sat him on a chair and stepped away, negotiating long and animatedly among themselves. Öcsike took pity on his old acquaintance and brought him a glass of rakija.

"I really don't drink anymore."

"I hear that the police stole your bicycle," said Öcsike.

Kalman turned up both his palms, to which Öcsike gave a disappointed scowl and spat on the floor.

"Fascist scum," he said, adding with particular irritation, "We alone must prove our honor."

At one point Kalman overheard Mika Šimunov, a former day worker and the oldest of them, telling Tucakov, a thirty-year-old unemployed blacksmith, and Štrangar, a thirty-five-year-old discharged machinist from the boatyard, that Kalman should be killed. "What do we want with that fool? Since he was struck by that lightning they say he talks to himself. And he wasn't exactly right in the head before! He'll be the end of us. He talks nonsense."

Scared, Kalman called out, "Come on, old Mika, you at least know who my father was."

That gave Mika Šimunov pause, and after a little more muttering they agreed to Kalman's offer. But Kalman's delight, or at least relief, was suddenly cut short. He would be on trial, they said; the smallest sign of betrayal and he would be liquidated —since there were comrades who would take revenge—as an example to anyone else who might consider doing the same. And they sat down with him at the same table and asked him to tell them everything he knew about the goings-on within the village authorities, showing the most interest in the particularities of the well-armed police and the situation at the synagogue where they were billeted. Kalman swallowed hard and started to sweat, realizing that, by dint of circumstance, he was once again in trouble, since he did not possess such information.

"Gentlemen..." he began.

"Comrades!"

"Comrades, I have to return to my afternoon round. And through the forest, so that no one sees me."

That took the comrades by surprise, but they had to agree that it would be unwise to behave suspiciously. They told him to be at Öcsike's at eleven that evening. Not the Tench, but Öcsike's actual house in tucked-away Danube Street. And so they finally parted, suspicious and unsettled, telling him once more to take care what he said and to whom.

Since the occupation, Öcsike worked only day shifts and left the nights to his young nephew, István. He had good reason, since the police would spend all night wandering from inn to inn, getting drunk and starting trouble under the pretense of security and the search for suspects, particularly communists. That's how many ended up in jail and all too often in forced labor in Hungary, from which some never returned. That's why the daytime meetings of the little conspiratorial group were held in the Tench, when everyone was out on business and the police officers were resting, and at Öcsike's place at night. Kalman knew very well where Öcsike lived, since one of his crossroads was there, the last one, the farthest away. Finishing work for the day, around eight o'clock, he decided to kill some time at The Duck over a glass of milk and a plate of strudel.

He anxiously holed himself up in a corner, since that evening the police happened to have gathered there too. Three of them. One always stayed at the base. And already at nine o'clock they were partying to the music. Crying "az a szép, az a szép" as the tamburitza players plucked their hearts out and picked up the money that the officers tossed on the floor.

"Dad, if you say we have to sharpen our nerves, then..." Kalman told the Voice and took a drink of milk to wash down a barely chewed mouthful of stale strudel that had gotten stuck in his throat. Worst of all was that his bicycle was parked outside the inn, together with Toza. He stole out at about a quarter to eleven and stopped at the bicycle and Toza, warmly greeting both. "That's animals for you—he can't help but love the bicycle to bits," Kalman said to the Voice.

Toza was thrilled to see him, wagging his tail so much that he knocked the leaning bicycle to the ground with a loud clatter. In a flash, two officers appeared and began shouting at Kalman. One even took out a pistol and fired into the air. Kalman fled into the night, seen off with a laugh and a few Hungarian expletives.

He reached Öcsike's at exactly eleven o'clock. Öcsike lived alone. His wife had run away a few years ago, so he said, and so the house always appeared empty. As it did then. So Kalman let himself in through the gate, reaching over the top to the key that hung from a string on the other side. He locked it behind him and headed inside. At the end of the long yard, he saw a pale light in the window of the summer kitchen. It was very quiet, so he slowly, cautiously approached the light. "What if they kill me?" he whispered to the Voice, and, stricken with fear, he opened the door a crack. The four comrades were sitting inside, illuminated by candles that stood on a low table. Tucakov and Öcsike held knives in their hands, but he quickly saw relief on all their faces. The comrades were actually a little angry at themselves, since Kalman's arrival had shown the amateurism in their organization. Where was the lookout? Where was the password? Tucakov said that in the event they were betrayed, the police would slaughter them like stray cats. A short but angry argument broke out. Even the knives came out once more—pure theatrics, but still—before old Šimunov dealt them a few teacherly slaps on the wrist and peace was restored. Back then people showed far more respect for their elders, at least in Siga, hence why Šimunov could feel confident enough to act in such a way. Kalman stood in a corner nervously watching everything that went on. When all the bitterness had subsided, they gestured to an empty seat and offered him a rakija. With great self-control he refused the drink, but sat down. Settling quickly, he answered all their questions about the affairs of the Village Hall, but most of all about the armed police unit. Kalman had discussed this a little with one of the guards, a step for which there was some understanding among those present, given they considered the seizing of Kalman's bicycle and dog a great injustice. However, it turned out that he was not really in a position to enlighten them very much, since the police were a story unto themselves and actually did not answer to anyone in Siga but in Sombor. Concerning the Village

Hall and its affairs, other than the fact there was no longer a warden but something called a mayor, there was no particularly relevant information to be had. Practical, everyday issues were dealt with in ways that were largely familiar. The only news was that on the establishment of the new authority in the Village Hall, ten rifles and five pistols were supplied. Four of the rifles were used by the Village Hall guards, locals who were entrusted with them each day and returned them at the end of their shift. Those four rifles were in circulation, while the other six, along with the five pistols, were locked in one of the back rooms that served as storage.

"We have to get our hands on those weapons!" Tucakov cried out excitedly, adding dolefully that no one ever achieved anything with a few knives.

He earnestly explained the obvious: that they should arm themselves well for the coming clashes. In fact, they felt relieved to have gotten something of use out of Kalman. With the questioning over, they began noisily discussing the ways in which they could get their hands on the weapons, constantly having to quiet each other down. The discussion went on for hours, but Kalman was restrained due to the difficulty he had in holding more than one conversation at once. The comrades were unable to come up with a serious plan, and the early-summer sun was already starting to rise when they decided to finish for the night. Then Kalman spoke up again, a little reluctantly, suggesting with some hesitancy a completely different tack: they should first steal a few hunting rifles, and only then think about other operations. Otherwise, how would they do it unarmed? Pondering this for a minute, everyone excitedly agreed, appreciating the pragmatic elegance of the idea. At the same time, however, the realization of such an objective scared them a little. So when Tucakov proposed that Kalman, who still could not be considered a full member of the conspiratorial group, should prove himself to his comrades by getting hold of a hunting rifle all by himself, everyone agreed, satisfied to have avoided any significant personal risk for at least a little while. They were only human, after all. With that settled, they quickly went their own ways, one by one, some through the gate, others through the kitchen garden, and Kalman had no opportunity or time to contest what had been decided and reopen the discussion. What's more, he was told not to turn up again without the rifle.

"It doesn't seem like a particularly smart idea," Kalman told the Voice, stepping through the fresh dawn air. "I'm not completely incapable," he added exhaustedly. He dropped his head and knitted his brow.

Over the next few days, Kalman went through the motions at work and listened to the Voice's plans in the cool of his home. The humidity was intolerable; without a bicycle, he returned every day worn out from beating his drum and soaked in sweat. As if he did not have enough on his plate, women gave him not a moment's peace. Ever since Kata Lorbach's visit when he lay unconscious, he was regularly attacked—real attacks, since they could not be described in any other way—by unknown women. To be fair, perhaps "unknown" is not the most precise description. He would have recognized them had they not ambushed so cowardly, in the dark! But the problem, of course, was not so much the women as the Voice, or rather its eyes, which Kalman believed to be all-seeing. Endless shame and discomfort would flow from him at the mere thought of coupling with a woman. Yet it was as if the Voice was egging him on, since Kalman would desperately, as if in agony, refuse categorically. "Out of the question!" he would say firmly. "Forget it!"; "I won't!"; "Never!"; even "Get lost!" Already, Kalman was able to adopt a harsher tone with the Voice, yet still obey him. It might briefly rock their otherwise functional symbiosis, but things would always return to normal. And so it happened, twice a month sometimes, that Kalman would be jumped by some woman, in his house or at some other opportune place. Were it not for this symbiosis, he certainly would not have resisted. He knew that much about himself; he considered himself a bon vivant. Yet here he was, struggling with these women, who, for some reason, without exception, were very large and older than him, and so physical conflict became a challenge.

One evening that summer, for example, after delivering the news, Kalman stayed out to listen to the live music at The Duck. The band was playing various Hungarian songs, and around midnight the now drunk guests began losing control, and Kalman decided to go home and get a good night's sleep, since who likes to be sober among a bunch of drunks? He always remembered his period of sleeplessness as a terrifying time and so now enjoyed sleep like never before. Permission to sleep occupied a special place in the complex relationship between Kalman and the Voice. That evening, Kalman arrived home around midnight, and as soon as he had closed the front door behind him, someone grabbed him around the neck. Someone very heavy, since Kalman fell to the ground like a branch chopped from a tree. The woman immediately straddled him and sat down on his flattened body. He felt her hot, rapid breath on his face and the characteristic warm smell of skin. She was also large, roughly his height, and with such big breasts that, in pressing his head to the floor, they totally immobilized him. Kalman put up as much of a fight as he could muster, but to very little effect, since he could only move his legs. He was particularly terrified to discover that her arms were stronger than his, which he was unable to raise off the floor. Only when she started to reach for his genitals and so let go of one of his arms could he try to push her off, but he did not have the strength. However, when he felt his member begin to betray him and to stiffen in her hand, with that one free arm he began to hit her on the back, in the kidneys, and then to the back of the head. When that didn't work, he began pulling her hair, but again to no effect. It was her determination that horrified him the most. That terrifying will and drive that had harnessed her entire body, in all its strength, felt almost supernatural. As if something possessed the body of this woman, which was now sinking beneath the confines of human dignity, oxidizing, burning in fever and emanating warmth, the body of an animal engaged as if in defense of its young. In a moment of desperation, when he already thought all was lost and that he would lose control over that part of himself as well, humiliated once more, Kalman had a sudden thought. Maneuvering his head beneath her pressing breasts, he created enough room to bite her. With all his strength, he sank his teeth into her soft, juicy flesh, and his body for a moment was freed. The woman screamed, jumped off, and Kalman quickly pulled himself up as the mildly salty taste of blood spread through his mouth.

He lifted a light wooden chair and said, "Not this time, fatty!"

They stood face to face, two panting silhouettes. The woman's breathing slowed, and, grabbing for her breast, she realized she was bleeding. Straight away she began to sob, then to properly cry, not so much out of pain but helplessness, before finally letting out a bitter scream and flying through the door like a witch into the night. On hearing her sobs, Kalman felt surprisingly sorry for her. Though he had lacked in his life any particular authority who could have taught him many important lessons about people, he nevertheless had in him enough empathy that he found her tears deeply distressing. The whole situation sickened him. "Because I won't do it in front of you," he yelled at the Voice. "I won't do it in front of you, got it?" He headed for the gate, from which with one hard tug he snapped off the string that held the key, like at Öcsike's, and stuffed it into his pocket. Then he searched through the big drawer in the summer kitchen and finally found the key to the front door of the house and put that one too in his pocket, determined that the doors would not remain unlocked; such were the times, unfortunately. Behind locked doors Kalman managed to compose himself, and all he then wanted was to fall asleep as soon as possible.

He woke early the next morning, sat on the veranda, and began thinking and talking. So, how to get his hands on a rifle? He recalled that Anton Klet had owned a hunting rifle, but it was anyone's guess what had become of it. Besides, one of the first tasks of the police unit was to confiscate all the weapons held by hunters of Croatian and Serbian nationality. They dared not take them from the Germans, choosing on the whole to leave them in peace. Not to mention the Hungarians. It should be said though that there was hardly any serious friction between the various nationalities of Siga. Of course, among the Hungarians and the Germans there were a handful who permitted themselves the odd jingoistic slip, but it was all so obviously tinged by opportunism or personal vendetta that no one ever searched for roots elsewhere. As a rule, they were thugs who quickly became bitterly disappointed that the new circumstances had not altered in the slightest the hidebound nature of Vojvodina's villages and so sought fulfillment by joining the armies of their mother countries and heading off to the front. The others, those of less adventurist spirit or valor, could satisfy themselves with a few inns that in principle practiced segregation between guests. Though, if someone of the wrong blood wandered into such an inn, rarely would they be thrown out. Most innkeepers, regardless of nationality, would not hear of segregation and served anyone with money in their pocket. The situation, therefore, was not intolerable, providing one did not have any direct business with the occupying authorities. But the supply of arms certainly was that kind of business. Kalman wondered whether to take a look in the house of Anton's widow. But what would he tell her? That he needed a rifle? What for? He wasn't even a hunter. But then, to steal from his late patron just to avoid questions really made no sense. At the end of the day, it was possible that the rifle was no longer around. So he quickly decided to seek another solution. He spent the next few days wrestling with all sorts of ideas milling around inside his head. Among them was the Voice's own idea, which he categorically refused. "Are you out of your mind? I'm no hero." But as the days passed, the failure to find a solution and the acoustic omnipresence of the Voice saw Kalman give greater and more seductive thought to the idea proposed by the Voice. "But how?" he would ask, his face contorted with uncertainty. "It's impossible!" All of a sudden, he began spending more time in the Village Hall, idling about for whole mornings and afternoons there between his rounds. He drank coffee or, in the absence of coffee, tea from caramelized sugar and chatted with Mihály and clerk Béla. They were both petty opportunists. Neither nurtured any real passion nor wickedness, but had simply taken a decision to extract as much from the situation as they could. They were far from full-blooded nationalists. After a period of more intense socializing and sitting around, they surreptitiously and perhaps completely naively shared with Kalman that they had begun dealing in flour and sugar and invited him to join them. They could do with another pair of hands and eyes, and why not, since they were "on the same side." Besides, there was plenty to go around. Though the expression on his face said something else entirely, Kalman accepted the offer. They were delighted and took Kalman the very next day to what was once the storehouse of the Sauerborn nobles, which the Village Hall had taken over management of before the war, though it remained unused. To the left of the door stood sacks of sugar, flour to the right. About fifty of each. Better he not know the details, they told him. His job, besides town drummer, was to keep track of every sack that went in or out. They gave him the keys and a notebook and told him to come every evening to count the sacks and write everything down neatly and precisely, including the date. Nothing more, nothing less. In return, he would get a sack of flour and one of sugar every month. On top of his regular pay, naturally. A confused look on his face, Kalman confirmed his agreement, shook hands with both men, and everything ended in a modest celebration at The Duck.

The next day, however, he was stopped in the street by Sándor Elgec, a veteran hunter and game warden, who asked if he would like to enroll in the hunting association. Elgec figured Kalman looked so startled for some other reason, so added that they needed armed people, competent hunters, since the new authorities had forbidden anyone who was not Hungarian (or German) from bearing arms. Though himself Hungarian, Elgec spoke of this discriminatory practice under his breath, ashamed of what was going on. "I'll give you a rifle straight away; you don't have to pay anything," he said. This pleased Kalman, who was surprised that the idea had not occurred to him already. He would have taken the weapon with open arms, but judging by the pained expression on his face, the Voice would not allow it. He said goodbye to Elgec, who was left a little confused as Kalman hurried away, calling out that he would be in touch the next day. "Why not, for God's sake? I'd solve the problem without any trouble," Kalman told the Voice, incredulous. But the Voice obviously had his own plans, which Kalman tried in vain to discredit. "Why wouldn't that count as revolutionary activity? Why make such a circus of it when it can be done without any risk whatsoever? A legal and registered rifle, and I could say that someone stole it from me!" The debate, intense and unrelenting, raged until the next day. Kalman simply grew tired and gave in under pressure. The key, as always, was his inability to get a break from the unabating

Voice. He could no more flee from the Voice than flee from himself. It was a never-ending torture.

A few days later, in the small hours of the night, Kalman set fire to the thatched roof of the Sauerborn storehouse and headed to the Village Hall through the dark surrounding streets. Lying in a ditch by the cobbled road, he watched the two guards talking and smoking in the dark in front of the gate. Soon they saw to the east the large red halo from the fire and heard the angry ring of the church bell. Quickly they scattered, and Kalman cautiously crossed the road, entered the yard of the Village Hall, and closed the gate behind him. Using a metal bar, he broke through the front door and then the door to the storeroom, wrapped six rifles and five pistols in a blanket, together with a few boxes of ammunition that he stuffed into a linen sack, and exited through the garden behind the building. Jumping over the fence, he reached the yard of a house and the parallel street, creeping carefully through the darkness. At home, he pushed the blanket with the weapons under the roof of what was once his hog house and ran toward the Sauerborn storehouse. There he encountered a mass of people trying to douse the flames, among them the apoplectic Mihály and clerk Béla. Only the police officers stood indifferently to one side, watching what was going on, smoking and talking among themselves.

"Where've you been? I sent for you!" Mihály shouted at Kalman and thrust a bucket of water into his hands.

Unable to think of an intelligent response, Kalman put his head down and doused the fire as if his life depended on it. "What do I tell them?" he asked the Voice in panic.

By the time the fire had been put out, there was little left of the storehouse. Empty and tired, the people walked around the charred remains and jostled for cups of water poured by the women. To the east, the sun was rising. Kalman approached Mihály, his mouth opening and closing in distress but saying nothing. He gesticulated, making little sense, and looked back at the scene of the fire.

"All right, all right, there'll be more flour and sugar. Go get some rest," Mihály told him, his tone conciliatory, and patted him on the shoulder.

Kalman obliged, eventually collapsing helplessly into bed. He woke a few hours later, gripped by fear. He quickly changed and left for the Village Hall. The guard at the gate looked serious and didn't say a word. Inside, Mihály and Béla were interrogating several suspects: Josip Forgić, a well-known prewar black marketeer; Rudi Takács, a Hungarian, but known in the district over as a dealer in flour, sugar, and oil; as well as two Gypsies whose names did the rounds after every theft. He knocked on the door of the office and entered just as Takács was being questioned; the other suspects were sitting in another room, watched over by the other guard. Mihály walked out with Kalman and left Béla to continue the interrogation. He handed over the news for the day and pointed to the broken doors of the storeroom.

"You see this? Someone really crossed the line. But we'll get them sooner or later," said Mihály. Seeing how flustered Kalman was, he patted him on the shoulder once more and tried to calm him. "Don't worry. You've nothing to feel guilty about."

And that was that. Absolutely no one suspected him of anything. This delighted him initially, but after a few hours, while on his morning round, Kalman began to wonder how it was possible that everyone considered him so harmless. And by the evening he was completely depressed by the impression others had of him.

Hear ye, hear ye!

Great success for the German Wehrmacht. Operation Barbaros-sa in full swing. Battle for Smolensk decided!

Communist bandits arrested in Batina, Zmajevac, Suza, Draž, Kopačev, and Bezdan. Trial begins tomorrow in Sombor!

Due to shortages, purchase price of flour and sugar goes up. Orders placed at the Village Hall!

Notified!

The next few days passed peacefully for Kalman, and he avoided any other additional activities. That, of course, applied above all to contact with his small conspiratorial band. Only when the initial hubbub over the fire and theft had died down did the tension in Kalman subside, and he decided to take action. It should be said that he did not feel at all comfortable keeping so many weapons in his house, no matter how well hidden they were.

"You left me to wait," Sándor Elgec told him when they ran into each other. "Do you want to be a hunter or not? The game are going to do us damage; something has to be done," he said worriedly.

"Mister Sándor, I don't have time. You know very well that I have obligations every day. I don't know when I'd have the time," Kalman replied.

A little disappointed, Elgec continued on down the street, adding as he went, "Where there's a will, there's a way, my dear."

Kalman saw no sense in further discussion with the Voice. But he still rued that missed opportunity, particularly now when he felt on his skin the danger of his act. He resolved to visit Öcsike at the Tench late one morning after his first round. The tavern was empty; he found him all alone, gutting fish by the water. As soon as Öcsike saw him, he dropped the fish and the knife, hastily washed his hands, and began to wipe them on a cloth hanging from a willow branch. He approached Kalman excitedly and, looking over his shoulder, said, "Fuck me, that was some fiesta!" Kalman asked that they go inside and headed straight for the doors of the tavern. There, he told Öcsike everything: that he had decided to take brave and constructive action, and how he hoped now that any cloud of suspicion had been lifted from him. "By all means! By all means, my good man!" replied the delighted Öcsike, hugging him and producing a bottle of rakija and two glasses. This time, Kalman simply pushed away the rakija with his hand, and Öcsike knocked back both. They quickly agreed on another meeting that very night and briefly discussed how best to move the arms to Öcsike's house. Everything suggested seemed to Kalman more dangerous than the most reliable method: that he simply carry them to Öcsike's house under cover of night. This was fine by Öcsike, since it meant less risk for him and the others, so he accepted the proposal and gripped Kalman's hand on parting, making clear how much he valued and respected his courage.

Kalman spent the rest of the day tense and expectant, every so often grudgingly confirming to the Voice that "yes, you were

IVAN VIDAK

right." But still he could not pull himself together and come to terms with events in which he had been the chief protagonist. He had the feeling that something unpredictable and toxic was baring its teeth at him from within that cycle of events, from that Sauerborn smoke. Some kind of fissure, so to say. Whatever the case, he met nightfall prepared. Waiting until it was completely dark, and then some more, he stole out to the hog house without a lamp to get the guns. He feared that even the lamp's faint glow might penetrate the pitch darkness and throw a treacherous light on the dramatic events of late, events that reverberated through a village so rarely the backdrop for such incidents. In the duration of that dark walk, his eyes grew used to the lack of light. By the time he reached the street, he could make out shapes perfectly and move freely. The only hiccup on the way was more symbolic than threatening: about halfway to Öcsike's house, he passed one of the police officers on the road, the one who had taken his bicycle, of course, and whom the loyal Toza followed as he had once followed Kalman. Kalman hid behind a pile of logs outside a house and watched. There was not, in fact, any need to hide, since the officer carried in his hand a lamp that barely penetrated the dark. On that bicycle, armed and accompanied by the dog, inside the aureole of hazy yellow light, he looked more like a mythological apparition than a genuine threat. All the same, the sight set Kalman's heart racing; something pressed at his chest and became lodged in his guts. "Sometimes it feels like you would be happiest if I were to lose everything," he told the Voice quietly. By then the shining apparition had moved on, and Kalman calmly arrived at Öcsike's house.

The company in Öcsike's summer kitchen had been eagerly awaiting him for some time. They were smoking and drinking, but the atmosphere was tense, absent of any real enjoyment. Losing his balance, Kalman tumbled through the door with a bang. Everyone popped up. But before anyone had the chance to react, Kalman laid the blanket on the table, knocking over glasses and whatever else was there. Then he breathlessly opened it and revealed to everyone the shining guns. He shook the ammunition from the sack.

"Well I'll be damned," said Stipan Tucakov, slurping bitter saliva from the soggy cigarette he held between his lips.

They began running their hands over the pile of weapons as if it were a young animal they dare not disturb.

"Six rifles and five pistols," Kalman said proudly. "That enough for you, my heroes?"

Öcsike immediately picked up a pistol, opened a box of ammunition, loaded up the cylinder, and held it out to Kalman. "This is yours. You earned it," he said importantly and patted Kalman on the back of the head.

The others nodded at this rather ceremonial moment before each of them approached Kalman and shook his hand. Kalman felt unexpectedly satisfied. Though from the start he had wavered over the entire undertaking and had initially favored a far less dangerous option with the hunting rifle, these expressions of respect triggered in him a degree of self-satisfaction, which is not to be scoffed at in moments of serious vacillation. After acknowledging his feat and now in a completely different mood, the comrades threw themselves on the weapons as if gripped by a fetish. They each took a pistol and wedged it into their belt without much inspection or familiarization, as if well versed in the tools of war. Then they turned excitedly to the rifles. Fascinated, they stroked them, turned them over, studied them, like orphans opening presents on Christmas morning. So captivated were they by their new and powerful possessions, it was as if they had been hypnotized. Their faces changed, and the longer they held the rifles in their hands, the less they resembled themselves. Soon, completely spontaneously, it was decided that they should practice shooting them. They would have happily unloaded a volley at the police right then, in the middle of the night, but of course they had to think smart, that was plain.

Mika Šimunov had a suggestion: his old friend Joza Čenga was a forester on the grounds known to everyone as the Štale, and it so happened that the Hungarians had not touched him, so he was still working there and living in a small, purpose-built log cabin that no one bothered to visit because the Štale were well out of the way. Who'd run into them there? The only people to go there were sent as a punishment. Not only would they be able to shoot, but Joza would shoot with them! But perhaps it would be sensible to take only the pistols, since who's going to lug rifles all the way there and back? That would be dangerous, one of them reasoned. That's right, agreed the others, but then what use are the rifles, what will the use be when the time comes if we don't know how to fire them? In the end it was the ever-agile Öcsike who stepped up and said that he would transport the rifles there and back, and hide them in the meantime. And that's how they parted, each with a fully loaded pistol in his belt. The fifth they left with Öcsike, together with the rifles and the remaining ammunition.

They hatched a plan to visit Joza Čenga at the Štale in two days' time. Kalman, however, very quickly realized that he would not be able to participate, due to his work obligations. Quite simply, he would not have time to go and come back in the break between his two rounds. You see, the Štale were a good few hours away by horse and cart, and when you put together the full journey, plus the time spent shooting, eating, and drinking, it was clear that the entire adventure would take up the whole day. So there was no question of Kalman collaborating in the outing, and he immediately let Öcsike know.

"No problem," Öcsike said. "And anyway, you're our operative for special operations. You're of more use to us here, at your post."

Kalman accepted this without much complaint, probably because those kinds of collective drinking binges—which was what it was really all about—had lost all attraction since he gave up alcohol.

That July 31 began like any other day: coffee in the Village Hall, taking receipt of the news, his morning round, and then off to The Duck for breakfast. "Why would I go?" he had said to the Voice the day before. "I'll practice another time." And then, "Don't push me around, please," accompanied by those old tics that for a long time were absent. This all meant that the Voice was pushing hard, and Kalman was resisting like a moody teenager. On the actual day of the operation, he was exhausted by the Voice, even wavering over whether to have a rakija while sitting in The Duck. Who knows how the day would have ended and where that pressure might have taken him, had a commotion not broken out around lunchtime in the center of Siga. All the police officers had gathered outside the Village Hall, armed to the teeth and agitated. Soon, from Sombor, there arrived a small truck carrying a handful of Honvéd, and together they set off in a cloud of dust in the direction of the forest. Nervous, Kalman hastily finished his afternoon round and headed for the Village Hall in the hope of finding out something. Mihály and Béla, talking animatedly and drinking wine, stood up with excitement when they caught sight of Kalman.

"Excellent news, my dear Gubica," said Mihály, offering him a seat. He told him how the night before, Tucakov had been drinking with a few of the village firemen in Lenđel's inn way out near the graveyard. And stupidly, completely out of the blue, as is often the way with drunks, he blurted out about the weapons, even showing off his pistol, and about the plan to go to the Štale. Kalman was not told who snitched on Tucakov, but given such recklessness—stupidity, really—it was hardly that important. First thing in the morning, Mihály went to the post office at Ilonka's and telephoned Sombor. Kalman was initially horrified by the news and, understandably, was frightened for himself. But it quickly became clear to him that he would have probably been the first to be arrested, had they known anything about him. He gradually caught his breath, but was still far from composed. Leaving the Village Hall, his drum over his shoulder, he began crisscrossing the village. "Dear God, what do I do now?" Kalman asked the Voice. "How can I do that? Save them? But that's crazy; they'll kill me on the spot," he said. But quickly, despairingly, almost in tears, he added, "If you say so..."

Kalman went home and, his hands shaking, ferreted out the pistol from under the roof of the hog house, stuffed it into his belt, and set off for the Village Hall. No sooner had he arrived and greeted the armed guards than he heard the engine of the truck on its way back. The truck, of course, needed dramatically less time than a horse and cart to get to the Štale and back, let alone by foot. The guards opened the gate and stood on the street to secure the truck's approach. The vehicle suddenly appeared and turned on the cobblestones directly into the yard of the Village Hall, leaving the guards to close the gate and secure the street. Kalman was also in the yard among the village officials who had gathered. He was so scared he could hardly breathe. He moved his hand under his shirt and gripped the gun. Tics made his pale face dance, and his other arm, hanging at his side, twitched as if electrified. That he was under the control of another's terrible will was never more obvious than at that moment. Why else would he place himself in such an irrational and dangerous situation? Quickly, the Honvéd tossed Tucakov, Öcsike, Štrangar, and Mata Šimunov from the truck as if they were sick and useless animals. It was quite apparent that all four had been badly beaten. They couldn't even stand, but lay helpless on the ground, gasping for breath like fish through dribbling, bloodied mouths.

As Kalman watched them, his eyes widened and his grip on the pistol tightened. He took a step forward then stopped, shifting his weight from one leg to the other. His breathing began to imitate that of his beaten comrades. He had only a few moments to survey the situation before the Honvéd brought from the truck the weapons they had seized and loaded on ten sacks of flour. Then in pairs they hauled each prisoner up by their armpits and dragged them back into the truck. "I can't," Kalman whispered tearfully, afraid to say anything among the enemies that surrounded him. "I might as well kill myself straight away; it's what'll happen anyway." And for the first time he disobeyed the Voice. In the end the group of Honvéd that had come by truck from Sombor escorted the prisoners to Bezdan for police interrogation, leaving the police in Siga to their regular work. Kalman stood in the street and watched, paralyzed, as the truck pulled away. He gradually loosened his grip on the pistol, and his concentration was finally broken by the sound of the gate closing. The last thing he saw behind the guard was Mihály shaking hands with Béla and giving him a satisfied wink.

"Kalman, come for a drink," Mihály called through the closed gate.

"I don't drink anymore. You know I don't drink," Kalman replied.

He went home in a kind of half-conscious trance and cried for an hour, for as long as he could before his evening round. He cried mostly for himself, understanding how close he had come to death. But the worst thing of all was that it was not all over: What if one of his comrades gave him up? After the evening round, careful not to bump into anyone but otherwise without much thought, Kalman began to run, his head pounding. He was completely unaware of anything around him. By the time he collected himself, night had fallen, and he found himself in dense forest on a dirt road leading to the Kazuk forest grounds. He stopped, looked around, and then turned and started heading back to Siga.

"Say what you want, but I should have taken that hunting rifle and then said it was stolen from me," he told the Voice. "How's what you came up with better? They're all in jail. I never should have listened to you; it was obvious there'd be problems," he said, his tone ever harsher. An anger had awakened in him, a sense of spite, and he began resisting with greater determination and force, repeating over and over, "They'd kill me like a dog," and "I won't," and "Never again," and "It's out of the question," and "Absolutely not." And when, in a fit of rage, he cried, "Fuck you, I won't!" he suddenly stopped, just short of Siga, having sensed something moving in the bushes at the roadside. His hand on the pistol grip, Kalman squinted through the darkness as a large woman tore from an elder bush and headed straight toward him. With surprising decisiveness, he brandished the pistol and pointed it at her. Fortunately, the weapon was not cocked, so having awkwardly worked the slide and loaded the chamber, he was composed enough to raise it into the air and only then fire off three rounds. Although he succeeded in frightening the dark figure and sending her into an ungainly flight, Kalman too leapt out of his skin. Panic-stricken by the noise of the gun, he fled in the opposition direction of the mystery woman.

IVAN VIDAK

4.

NOTHING HAPPENED. In spite of the battering meted out, the comrades kept their mouths shut, and no one asked Kalman anything. A month after the incident, he was finally able to relax and stop looking over his shoulder. He could sleep again. Though it was rough that month, really rough, particularly since there were more arrests in Siga and the surrounding area; in trucks, they picked up and drove off anyone deemed remotely suspicious, without relent. Then everything stopped, a calm descended. The beast had had its fill. People even began slowly returning from Hungarian casemates, going back to work and licking their wounds in silence. But not Kalman's comrades. After a trial in September, Stipan Tucakov and Öcsike were sentenced to ten years in prison, Adam Štrangar to fifteen, and old Mika Šimunov to nine months. Tucakov would die in prison in Budapest in 1943. Öcsike was in all probability beaten to death right at the start, since he was never heard from again; the fact he was Hungarian probably irritated them even more. November 1942, Adam Štrangar and some 800 other prisoners from Bačka were sent under military guard to serve out their sentences in forced labor on the Eastern Front. There they would witness the collapse of the German line at Stalingrad in January 1943, after which they joined the Red Army. In summer 1944, they would link up with the 1st Yugoslav Tank Brigade under the Red Army, in whose ranks they would return to Yugoslavia by tank at the end of the war. Mika Šimunov would endure ten months in Szeged's Csillag prison and return home at the end of spring 1942. He lost all interest in revolutionary operations. His age would catch up with him.

It should be said that Kalman at that time became slightly withdrawn. A rift emerged between him and the Voice, a loss of trust, since Kalman could not escape the conclusion that the whole circus never would have happened had he not listened to the Voice. After all, that was what he had told him, swore at him, at the very beginning. And now, with the dust settled to a degree, he was seriously considering giving up his revolutionary involvement. Even if he wanted to continue, could he do it alone? His comrades were no longer around, and he had no other contacts of his own. He wanted to take things easy, do his job, watch movies, maybe even fish. "Perhaps opportunities will come along, but I don't know if that's something I really need," Kalman told the Voice during that time. The Voice appeared not to force the issue, as if saving him for better days, and Kalman spent the whole autumn fishing. Like some spent veteran, he passed the day between shifts sitting on the banks of the Old Danube, hypnotized by the float. Occasionally he would pull out the odd bleak, rudd, or bream, but he showed no great delight, as if it was nothing but a distraction from observing the float. Since he never was taught the skill of fishing, not even when he spent so much of his time on the water, it would appear he learned from the Voice: from placing the worm or bread paste onto the hook to mystically watching the quiet dance of the float on the water, which was the one sight that brought him calm. With late autumn and the arrival of winter, time on the water became less comfortable, so Kalman took to pursuing another of his wishes: he went to a movie. A long time had passed since he last saw one, and he had high expectations, dashed, unfortunately, by the disappointing Hungarian romantic comedy he watched about a harlot out to snare a husband, particularly because of his complex relationship with women since the arrival of the Voice. Though, hand on heart, the relationship had never been a simple one. But only after the film did the evening really show its hand.

Leaving with another twenty people from Janika Kovács's house, where movies were shown at that time, the light in the yard suddenly went out, the generator fell silent, and a loud commotion ensued. Through that confused noise Kalman suddenly heard the pained whine of a dog somewhere in the crowd. Without thinking, he pushed his way through and found Janika, lamp in hand, and the officer with the bicycle viciously beating Toza because the poor animal had peed on the generator. Right before Toza's intervention, Janika had clumsily poured more fuel into the generator. It was all wet and flammable, and when a spark flew a very small fire broke out and was quickly doused, but the damage was done—the generator was broken. The bicycle had been leaning against the wall right beside the generator, and anyone who knew Toza and how he never left the bicycle's side could have expected nothing else. But who's going to have understanding for a dog? The scene so pained Kalman that he was shaking; he felt like he was being stabbed in his ears every time Toza yelped in pain. Kalman leapt on Janika and began hitting him, probably reasoning that it was less risky than hitting the officer. This flash of rationality proved completely futile when another officer suddenly appeared, and the two guardians of the peace began laying into Kalman in the middle of the yard with whatever they could find. One of the bystanders had the presence of mind to call Mihály, who lived a few houses down and who quickly turned up and stopped Kalman from being beaten to death, less on account of his authority than his appeals for mercy.

Bloodied, Kalman heard and felt one of the officers spit on him before they withdrew. He about pulled himself onto all fours, enough to cast a glance at the bicycle and Toza, who was cowering against the wall, struggling for breath and bleeding from his muzzle. And yet, when the officer took the bicycle and started to push it away with his colleague, Toza appeared uncertain but followed it nonetheless. The officer tried to shoo him away, swore at him, kicked out at him, but poor Toza could not help himself and limped after the bicycle from a safe distance. Once the officers and Toza had disappeared from sight, a few of those present helped Kalman to his feet and got him home. Sitting on his bed, he thanked them and asked to be left alone. Once they left, he shuffled to the well in the yard and, with great difficulty, pulled up a pail of cold water that he dumped down his throat like he had just returned from a desert march. Then he tottered to the hog house, dug out the pistol hidden under the roof, and stuffed it into his belt. He had been carrying that pistol everywhere, especially at night, but that evening he had forgotten it. Fortunately so, perhaps, since who knows what would have happened had he been armed? Summoning his last ounce of strength, he returned to bed, checked the gun was loaded, and laid back, slowly, painfully, clutching the pistol to his chest, before falling asleep.

Due to the swelling on his face, he spent the next few days squinting and slurring. The pain in his bones and joints, from bruising and perhaps even fractures, lasted almost the whole winter, and only the warmth of the stove provided any relief. Luckily, Kalman had gotten hold of enough wood that winter that he did not have to seek out the warmth of the village inns, sparing him the pain caused by the worst of his wounds: shame. He avoided other people as much as possible and nothing, other than his work, got him out of the house. His drumming was quiet and ungainly—crippled, one could say—and hardly passed muster. He ate lunch at the Village Hall by paying one of the guards to pick up food for him at The Duck. He imagined encountering those faces at the inn—faces that lived to sneer, to gossip, to revel in the misfortune of others—and wishing the earth to open up and swallow him. Those he met in the street, he had to endure, but he could get away swiftly, sidestepping them as far as he could, and, if that was too painful, dropping his gaze. Kalman knew very well that he would not be able to stay away from people forever, but it would be enough to keep to himself, as much as possible, until his body healed. Later he would marvel at his strength of will, not realizing that to flee from misery poses no great challenge for a man's determination. Anyway, he saw out the winter.

In March 1942, strong and fit, hair brushed, and dapperly dressed, Kalman hurried toward the church, asking the Voice, "Are you completely sure?" It turned out that a new, young parish priest, Matiša Zvekanović, had arrived in Siga. In all likelihood, Kalman was the first to find out, given that when he arrived at the Parish House, the young priest, in his late twenties, had only just pulled his cases from the horse-drawn carriage that had brought him from the railway station.

Two elderly nuns helped with his lighter belongings. Next to him stood the bell ringer, old Marijan "Lacika" Jelić, and the even older housemaid, Roza, whose job was to cook, clean, and tidy up for the priest. These two members of what one might call the support staff stood watching in confusion as Kalman crossed the broad courtyard of the Parish House between its ancient and imposing chestnut trees. The courtyard was enclosed by the church, the parish office and apartment, the outbuildings, including Roza's quarters, and the lodging for the two nuns who served there in the St. Peter and St. Paul's Church. Matiša only noticed the newcomer when Kalman drew quite near and stopped in front of him, nervously wringing his hands. Matiša stepped forward warmly and offered Kalman his hand, believing him to be another member of the welcoming committee.

"This is our town drummer, Kalman," said Lacika.

"Ah, Kalman! Pleased to meet you, pleased to meet you, praise be to the Lord and to you," Matiša said heartily, gripping his hand, while Lacika and Roza regarded the nervous Kalman with suspicion and some concern.

Finally Kalman spoke as well, hushed and conspiratorially, saying he needed to talk to him most urgently. Matiša was caught slightly off guard by the sudden seriousness and began looking around in confusion, seeking some instruction in the looks of the others. When he got none, he had little option but to ask Kalman inside, without knowing exactly where it was he was inviting him. That was when Lacika came to his aid by taking a suitcase in each hand and telling the priest to follow him. Together they surveyed the interior, which Matiša was seeing for the first time and Kalman could barely remember. The situation was more than a little bizarre, and Matiša swiftly gave up on familiarizing himself with the space and, as soon as they entered the office of the parish priest, settled himself into a comfortable armchair beside a large oak table and gestured to Kalman to sit opposite on an ordinary yellow stool of the kind one might find at a bar.

"Tell me, my friend, what can I do for you?" asked the priest.

"How can I say..." Kalman began.

"Tell me, speak freely; I'm listening."

After a prolonged pause, Kalman summoned the courage and told Father Matiša that he knew of the priest's role in "our thing" and that before his arrival he had visited Kalman's comrades in prison. Startled, Matiša went white and mumbled something about being confused and not quite understanding what he was getting at, but Kalman would not be derailed and peppered him with questions as if the priest had already confirmed everything Kalman had set out before him. Were there any messages? What should be done next? Will someone take over? When the priest realized that Kalman would not be deterred, the expression on his face changed in a flash. He stood up and looked sternly into the corridor before closing the door to the office.

"How do you possibly know this?" he asked.

Kalman blurted out something about not being able to say, that he simply knew and that it was of vital importance that he tell the priest everything because he was terribly worried. "Because, you see, I'm one of them," he said. "I'm surprised they didn't mention me."

"Come to dinner, today, after evening Mass. Mrs. Roza has already announced a feast in my honor, and there's no point in me going through it alone. So, tonight. You can see for yourself that it's all a bit hectic right now," said Matiša, visibly perturbed.

Just then, Lacika knocked on the door with his hands full of baggage. Faced with a fait accompli, Kalman had no choice but to withdraw, deeply suspicious and irritated. As he ambled away in the direction of the Village Hall, he said to the Voice, "It wouldn't be the first time you've gotten me into trouble."

Hear ye, hear ye!
Another Japanese victory in the Pacific!
Australia declares war on Thailand, Japan responds with bombs!
Rudolf Rosenberg leases his hemp mill in Karlica to businessman Jacob Herman from Prigrevica!
Notified!

Straight after his evening round, Kalman, still dressed up from the morning, took his drum back to the Village Hall and set off for the Parish House. The priest was waiting for him in

IVAN VIDAK

the large dining room where a feast had been laid out, lavishly illuminated by candles and lanterns, while a fire crackled happily in the oven stove, defying the stubbornly cold March night. Matiša was drinking a full-bodied local red wine from a crystal glass and leafing through a large brown leather-bound book at a small table beside the stove. Under Roza's suspicious gaze, Kalman was taken into the dining room, where the priest greeted him warmly and instructed Roza that the dinner could now be served. During the brief wait for the food, the priest offered Kalman wine, invited him to sit, and talked to him of prosaic, practical matters concerning the affairs of the church. There was none of the conspiratorial tension of their parting. Kalman carefully clutched the crystal glass, regarding it from all sides, marveling at the ruby refraction of light and clearly giving away the fact that he had never before held such a glass. Having satisfied his curiosity, he returned the glass to the puzzled priest and remarked that he no longer drank. Dinner was quickly served, and Matiša invited Kalman to sit at the table, where roast duck glistened in front of them, accompanied by potatoes and small bowls of beetroot and sauerkraut.

"You'll forgive my caution, but it couldn't be helped," Matiša said after dinner, reclining in the armchair and lighting his pipe. He admitted that he'd heard of Kalman, had been directed to him, truth be told, by Tucakov, who had dubbed Kalman as a person of trust, a man of a specific character, dependable. Tucakov had even sent Kalman an apology. But Matiša had been startled by the fact that Kalman already knew everything. "Before your arrival, however, Roza happened to mention that others here in Siga knew that I'd visited the prisoners, due to Tucakov's wife having only visited her husband the day before."

Matiša did not share with Kalman that Roza had also mentioned to him the town drummer's reputation in Siga, and how he had been brutally beaten by the police last year.

Kalman was happy with how things were turning out, astonished once more at the Voice and his ability to complicate everything. While he deliberated how the authority his father held over him was irrevocably crumbling, Matiša pensively told him that hard times lay ahead. He immediately dropped to his knees in front of a religious picture and invited Kalman to pray with him to the Father.

"The Father knows all and will help us," said Matiša.

"True, he knows, but it's questionable whether he'll help," Kalman replied.

"There's always hope," the priest concluded.

Kalman did as he was asked, though he was not sure why. The pair kneeled before the Father, the Son, and the Holy Spirit.

The instructions Kalman received over the following days in conversation with Matiša were not particularly encouraging. In the purges of Siga over the past year, the National Liberation Movement, the Partisans resistant to the occupying Axis powers led by Josip Broz Tito, had been wiped out. The instruction was to mobilize anew, but with great discretion, and then wait for an opportune moment. That was the instruction from more than one source, from comrades in Subotica and in Sombor who had withstood the purges and continued operations from deep underground. The concrete task assigned to Kalman was to recruit at least two new members to the National Liberation

Movement, in order for the Siga branch to act effectively when the moment came. Back then Kalman could not have known that that moment would only come around 1944, but it was as if he sensed it, since the feeble outlook laid out before only served to sour his mood completely. That is, perhaps not Kalman, but certainly the Voice.

Kalman continued to spend time on the water, fishing, wandering through forests, and marveling at nature and animals like some Francis of Assisi, but the Voice demanded action. Always and only action. He spoke as if there was no time to lose, like the ground was burning under his feet and he was gripped by restlessness. Though there was a war going on, the average resident of a remote village under occupation, such as Siga, could wipe that fact from his or her mind, since before long there was no great difference between life in peacetime and life in the clutches of war. Poverty was anyway widespread. The war simply did not show itself in the people of Siga, while life of course did not stop, so someone who lived only in the moment could very easily argue that there was peace, not war—for the simple reason that everything in Siga really was peaceful.

If, over the next two years, there was a battle between Kalman and the Voice, it would be a battle between peace and war. Dialectically, absolutely, since Kalman and the Voice could not get away from one another, like a hammer and anvil, destined to wear each other down. And since for two years no particular operations had been undertaken, the Voice lost patience and began digging his heels in and stirring confrontation within Kalman where there should have been none. Kalman became a wall that should be toppled in order to reach the battlefield.

It's not black, but white; not tomorrow, but today; not up, but down: the Voice contradicted him on everything, splitting him into pieces and creating an explosive charge of immense force.

So 1942 passed peacefully, at least on the surface. Neither Kalman nor the Voice managed to come up with a way to recruit anyone to the National Liberation Movement. People wanted to live in peace, and if it was at all possible to bury their heads in the sand, they buried them. Kalman initiated Matiša into the small smuggling operation with flour and sugar that Mihály had originally gotten him into. New storage was found, at the Village Hall, under armed guard. Mihály and Béla feared nothing, and everything proceeded apace as it had before the Sauerborn storehouse was razed. Receiving a sack of flour and a sack of sugar every month, Kalman already had a growing stockpile in his house, and, only when he noticed he would soon run out of space, it occurred to him that something should be done with it—wonder of wonders! The parish priest's face lit up when he laid eyes on the sacks. Such a stockpile could make many things a lot easier and open many doors, he said. So they agreed to transfer the sacks by night to the Parish House, where new sacks would also be delivered, and the priest would manage the capital in the interests of their common goal. They considered whether to simply pay people to join the National Liberation Movement (the Voice's idea, of course), but the priest swiftly rejected this. Something else was missing, some kind of material motive—a moral hook, so to say. And that's precisely what came along in the spring of the following year.

Many years later, Milenko Beljanski, the founder and director of the *Sombor News*, would describe the event thus: "April

1943, Serbs, Croats, Slovaks, and Ruthenians were driven into forced labor with the Hungarian army. They were sent to Hungary, deep into Transylvania; some were transported to the Eastern Front. Those rounded up remained in civilian clothes; on their left arms they wore the red, white, and green of the Hungarian flag, and on their heads the Honvéd hat. They were not paid for their work; they enjoyed a degree of freedom of movement and were able to visit home; at work they were watched by soldiers. They worked on the lands of Hungarian counts, in industrial firms, on the railways, the roads, and the mines; they built military installations, loaded and unloaded goods onto and off lorries and wagons; the fascistized Hungarian bourgeois did not have much use for the munkások (a Hungarian word meaning 'workers'). But in the summer of '42, when Hungary sent to the Eastern Front 200,000 young souls, holes were left in the workforce, and the solution was found in the mobilization of civilians. Their call-up as munkások was linked to both political and military developments; so that a large number of Bačka residents would not be in the vicinity of operations by the Yugoslav National Liberation Army, and would not enlist in its units, it was the corresponding and occasional policy of the occupier to keep them far from their homes and, as munkások, produce something. Hence many Siga villagers born between 1901 and 1916 found themselves subjected to forced labor, from which some returned after five or six months, others after twenty."

As is often the case, it was in this misfortune that Kalman and the parish priest found hope for their cause. As each unlucky fellow was taken away to join the ranks of the munkások, the priest would visit their family and offer them spiritual comfort but also, and most important, money and provisions. A form of bribery, no doubt, but the circumstances were extraordinary. Sometimes Kalman would accompany Matiša on these visits, since Mihály posed no real threat: he worried only about his own purse. He cared as much for the dirt under his fingernails as for what Kalman did with his own earnings and his reasons for visiting the poor with the priest. Particularly after the German and, consequently, Hungarian misery endured at Stalingrad. Word of this, albeit via unofficial channels, had reached those whom it was supposed to reach. And so it seemed that Mihály and Béla grew thirstier for more, grabbing ever faster for what they could, conscious that time for them was quite possibly running out. This suited Kalman and the priest, since their earnings also grew proportionately. But, even though they had the means, weapons could not readily be bought. The Voice considered this important, and Kalman in his own way passed it on to the priest. Matiša was not in favor of arms and was reluctant to talk about them, though he knew that wars are waged with weapons. He believed it was not the job of a parish priest to participate in violence. During 1943, people increasingly took courage and broke ranks, and there the priest found space for himself. He began cooperating with youngsters in preparing a theater play in Croatian, which was held in the Lenđel coffeehouse. Later they took an expanded repertoire to Santovo in Hungary, where local Croats, despite being on true Hungarian territory, openly spoke Croatian. A scandal erupted, and they were banned from further performances, but there were no other repercussions. Matiša considered this the best form of action, but for the Voice, and so too Kalman (who rather enjoyed theater), it was not concrete enough. In December 1943, news about the second session of the Anti-Fascist Council for the National Liberation of Yugoslavia appeared in the Croatian *Our Newspaper*, which was published in Sombor and was launched by Dr. Grga Vuković, a deputy in the Hungarian parliament. The text carried the most important part of the official Yugoslav news agency statement, and since it concerned a legitimate publication delivered even to the Village Hall, the Voice glimpsed an excellent opportunity. Clerk Béla usually prepared the news for Kalman, a job he had become well and truly tired of over the past year. So when Kalman, holding a copy of *Our Newspaper*, suggested that he himself prepare the news, Béla seized on it as the chance for a long-overdue holiday, feeding his hope that Kalman would one day take on the task full-time.

Hear ye, hear ye!

Prices of flour and sugar continue to rise!

The church launches a soup kitchen; the poorhouse does not have enough. Address the nuns!

In the movie theater, a new Hungarian romance!

Second session of the Anti-Fascist Council in Jajce; its legislative and executive body forbids the return of King Petar to Yugoslavia!

The National Committee is founded as a temporary Partisan government; its president is Tito, who has been given the title of marshal!

Debts run up abroad by the exiled government will not be recognized!

The Yugoslav peoples will decide on the political system of the state after the war!

Notified!

Kalman's news caused quite the stir, the biggest since the April the war started. The authorities showed no curiosity whatsoever for what Kalman shouted about. Interesting, in particular, because he first shouted the news in Croatian and only then in Hungarian. It was noticeable that many of those Hungarians who at first had no great issue with the occupation were slowly losing their illusions and leaning toward some other solution. Nevertheless, already in the spring the occupier gave notice that, even wounded, it could be very dangerous and that nothing was over yet. On April 26, 1944, police officers seized Siga's three remaining Jews—Armin Weinberger, a trader and landlord; his sister, Katarina Weinberger; and Sidonija Vámoser, née Engelmann, the mother of Ervin Vámoser, a local landowner who lived with his family in Klisa. None of them would return after the war.

At that time, there began almost daily Allied flights over Siga. Showing no mercy, they bombed Hungary over Admiral Miklós Horthy's decision in April that year to allow the Germans to enter, but over Siga they dropped only leaflets in Serbo-Croatian and Hungarian, calling on the enemy to surrender and informing the rest of the population about the Allied successes and developments in the war. People were very interested in the leaflets, reading them openly, without fear, and discussing them in the streets and inns. The atmosphere unnerved Kalman: they remained under occupation, but it was being enforced quite feebly, and the whole thing seemed to be suspended midair, ominous and indeterminate. A slightly strange situation, neither here nor there, without direction or destination, like a lethargic neurasthenic.

One scorching August day, Kalman wandered off in the direction of the Great Bačka Canal, where he fished in the fields toward Sombor, trying to relax and not listen too much to the Voice's plans, when his attention was drawn by the noise of planes. That was not, of course, particularly unusual during those months, but this time he was witness to a full-blown dogfight in which a German hunter took down a British four-engined Halifax bomber. Kalman followed as it slid through the air, trailing smoke behind it, and watched as six men parachuted clear before the plane struck the ground somewhere in the distance and exploded. Dropping his reed fishing rod into the water, Kalman began running toward the spot where he guessed he would find the airmen. He didn't find them immediately, but later, as he stood in a field of clover and looked with fascination at the torched wreckage, he saw two flares go up. One was more to the west, while the other was clearly fired from his immediate vicinity. He headed for a lone copse between the fields and found two pilots, one of whom was hurt. The other, propping up his wounded colleague, tightened his grip on his pistol but did not point it at Kalman, whom he recognized as a civilian. "Tito, Tito!" he said to Kalman, pulling out a map and pointing to the wooded, hilly region of Fruška Gora, which was a stronghold of the Partisan National Liberation Movement. Kalman glanced briefly at the map but only shrugged his shoulders, helplessly, and waved a few times in the direction of the east, as if to suggest it was far away. At that moment four other crew members approached, none of them hurt. Kalman's hands clenched as he listened to both the Voice and the cacophony of incomprehensible English in which the only thing he could make out was anxiety. Feeling aurally bombarded, he wanted only to disappear. The next moment, he turned and began running frantically toward the canal in which he had left his fishing rod. Stumbling over the bumpy furrows in the fertile, black land beneath the clover, he heard shouts and then a few shots. One round tossed up a clod of earth, and Kalman breathed in the dust. But, fortunately, he was not hit. Most likely, they wanted only to scare him into stopping, since they were as unnerved and frightened as the fleeing local. Or perhaps they did want to hit him, who knows? In moments of fright, anything is possible.

Kalman did not retrieve his fishing gear, but followed the canal to Siga, panting all the way. He headed straight for the Village Hall. "Are you completely sure?" he asked the Voice. "Aren't we on the same side?" But the Voice had made his call, and Kalman reported everything to Mihály, who immediately went to inform the police. Kalman, however, was not completely reconciled to the decision, which ate at him and roused the suspicion that surfaced after every one of the Voice's decisions that he followed through on. So Kalman sought relief in the universal solution in such circumstances: to seek approval. He went straight to Father Matiša and released a torrent of words about what he had done.

IVAN VIDAK

"Why, for God's sake?" the incredulous priest asked. "We're on the same side."

Kalman rambled on, veering between the reasons he had heard and the ones he himself had invented. It was hard to say which were more unconvincing. Since if the reason was not that they were not Russians, then the reason was the bad timing: the Partisans were nowhere to be seen, and what would they do with six Englishmen? Where to put them? Were they worth the danger and the risk of exposure? He driveled on and on, like a slave to sin, part of a demimonde in which reasons are always in the service of passion, never sense, and so seem deformed and foreign, almost perverse.

"My dear friend, it's a mystery to me who taught you sense," the deeply disappointed priest said with a sigh. "You could have simply left them to their fate and not sinned like this."

Kalman did not reject the criticism. He felt tired, squeezed dry, and spent like pomace at the bottom of a barrel. Matiša's criticism exposed what Kalman already sensed deep down: that his little symbiosis had entered a new phase in which it was hard to differentiate between what he heard and what he thought. He had become some kind of combination of himself and the Voice, son and father. It reminded him of those days of torture when the Voice first surfaced, when he had to drink himself silly to snatch a few hours' sleep. He was unsure whether the recollection was a sign of the continued autonomy, however great, of his being, or was little more than a threat. And that uncertainty only fed the fear that he was becoming some kind of amalgam of himself and something foreign, something unknown. He was sickened by the scene he witnessed the next morning, when the police escorted the six Allied airmen down the main street before they were taken to Sombor by German military truck. But the nausea did not last long.

As 1944 trundled on bleakly, so Kalman's excesses—not so much damaging as irrational and out of place—became more and more frequent. For example, with the police increasingly discreet and rarely seen at night, Kalman began stopping by the Tench once more. It had been run for some time by Öcsike's nephew, István, and the ambience and spirit of the inn had changed considerably. So, despite the fact that Kalman still was not drinking—though it had often occurred to him recently to start again—he was warmly welcomed, but stood sullenly at the bar and looked for someone to quarrel with. No one wanted to go up against him, for several reasons. Many already knew he was playing for more than one team, though the phrase could not be applied with its full force, given that his opportunism was more coincidental than premeditated and could even be considered positive. So, at the Tench, enthusiasm for his presence waned. Kalman would also occasionally visit Kata Lorbach. She had been left somewhat exposed, since by the second half of 1944 the Nazis of Siga had been scattered across Europe's front lines, and her inn was very often empty. The atmosphere was far from what it had once been. Kalman would take a seat at the bar, order some kind of juice, and sit there staring intrusively at Kata for twenty minutes, never saying what he wanted. Kata, of course, found this terribly unnerving, but she did not dare throw him out; she would serve him discreetly, saying little, and wait for him to leave. By late summer, early autumn, rumors were doing the rounds in Siga about who was with the

Partisans and their links. Fueling the gossip were individuals who in one way or another had suffered as a result of time spent as munkások or from some other misfortune and who were called to join up with the National Liberation Movement. The more the movement grew, the more intensely information did the rounds.

Since the night he had fired his gun, the onslaught of unknown women had stopped. Kalman swore he constantly encountered their imposing shadows, observing him, stalking him from dark corners, sometimes close enough for him to feel their breath, but there was no concrete contact. From time to time he felt them watching him through the windows of the inn, popping up from the street in a flash like true spies while he wiped the condensation from his glass with wet palms. Once he woke up terrified by what sounded like someone galloping across the thatched roof. Gripping his pistol, he went out into the yard, but nothing—not a soul. Whatever it was, he considered it best to remain on alert. Only in September, when he no longer allowed himself to be separated from his pistol at all, even during the day, did he find some peace, at least as far as that was concerned.

September provided the backdrop for another important event that would consolidate the National Liberation Movement in Siga. On the sixth of the month, Kalman was invited to a meeting in the office of the parish priest. Besides the priest, already there were his three most reliable local collaborators: Stipan "Bell Ringer" Marijanović, Ivan Pašić, and Ivan Škarica. Father Matiša was planning a trip to Subotica for all five of them on September 8. The occasion was a meeting with "Bata," a high-ranking member of the National Liberation Move-ment, and a final agreement on the armed operations that were undoubtedly approaching. Matiša emphasized that there were no obstacles to the trip going ahead, other than Kalman's town drummer duties. In fact, in saying this he hoped to talk Kalman out of accompanying them, since he had finally begun to fear his peculiar and often unpredictable behavior. The priest would like nothing more than to completely exclude him from the organization, but how, when Kalman carried the greatest authority as practically the original resistance fighter? Matiša was also a little uncomfortable with Kalman's sometimes pronounced predilection for bolshevism, communism—the influence of the Voice, no doubt. Maybe it was completely declarative, on paper only, but still.

Kalman, however, not giving it a second thought, shot back that there was no problem at all; let Mihály deal with it. He was off to Subotica! Faced with such decisiveness, Matiša ditched the idea of somehow shunting Kalman to the margins. It was not the right moment, and why would he expose himself to such perfidious machinations? Let it be how the good Lord decides. After all, he liked the lad. He was just a little difficult. At dawn on September 8, they gathered in the courtyard of the Parish House, loaded themselves and their things onto Marijanović's carriage, and set off. The journey was very pleasant. They chatted, ate, and drank, and it was as if everyone relaxed and opened up for that stolen moment out of their lives, when there was nothing to do but wait, as if for the rain to stop. Marijanović drove the carriage and took care of the horses, but was constantly turning around to take part in the conversation. Next to him sat his friend Pašić, a pig keeper and pauper from the lowest order of society. Škarica, the priest, and Kalman sat in the back on straw bales covered with blankets. It was a comfortable ride that allowed the passengers to forge bonds and relax. When they arrived in Subotica, the day was already drawing to a close, and the bells were ringing for evening Mass. In the Skenderović house they knew Father Matiša well, since he had often visited under the pretext of attending church assembly meetings. That was the justification for Croats from various parts of Bačka to gather there, but not necessarily led by their parish priests, since not all parish priests were the same.

The team from Siga was last to arrive, and the meeting was about to start; the carriage and baggage were attended to, and they were invited into the house. They were taken into a fairly large room in which fifteen peasants were sitting on chairs around a man in a Hungarian Honvéd uniform. Each of those present regarded this suspicious scene with consternation, cautious and uncertain, as if ready to run at any moment. When the men from Siga sat down too, as dumbfounded as the rest of them, the man in the Honvéd uniform introduced himself as Bata and opened the meeting. Without much else in terms of an introduction, Bata straight away began speaking about the evidently imminent fascist collapse, about the anticipation of freedom and the tasks that would have to be undertaken in order to get there. But then Kalman, with those clenched hands and facial tics, stressed the obvious: Why would any of those present believe a member of the Honvéd? His words were met with swift approval around the room. Only Matiša, who was sitting next to him, tugged him by the sleeve. It was as if he was the only one not put out by the Honvéd uniform. Bata stood and began explaining how the uniform was only camouflage, the same as his conspiratorial name, and, glancing quickly at the clock, asked for their patience for another ten minutes, and he would prove he was on their side. Of course, everyone impatiently and agitatedly asked what it was that would happen in ten minutes.

"Comrades, at exactly twelve o'clock, the electricity station in Subotica will be blown to pieces," said Bata.

That shut everyone up quickly; those with watches looked at them, and there began a somewhat bizarre ten-minute silence, interrupted only by the sound of loud breathing, coughing, the scraping of chairs, and the rumbling of someone's stomach. And true enough, at exactly twelve o'clock the thud of an explosion was heard somewhere in the distance and had an almost cathartic, relaxing effect on those gathered. They all stood in celebratory fashion and, amid a babble of voices, began milling around the room, approaching Bata and shaking his hand, slapping one another on the back, even hugging like delighted children. The meeting resumed with everyone in a good mood and highly motivated. In the end it was agreed that each group would receive that day ten rifles, and that their primary task would be the liquidation of the occupying force and the establishment of the people's authority. There then followed the formal enrollment of many of them into the Party. The meeting ended with a modest meal—something cooked up over a fire behind the house and washed down with the host's homemade wine—and they all went to bed, overcome either by the wine or fatigue. In the morning each group received their promised rifles, ten pieces wrapped in sheets, and a smallish wooden case full of ammunition. The Siga men hid theirs under the straw from the bales they had sat on on their way there and began the journey back.

On October 8, the occupying forces ordered an evacuation, because the Soviets had crossed the Tisa, and Partisan units from Šajkaš, Novi Sad, Bačka Palanka, Subotica, and Sombor were active across a large part of Bačka. In Siga, chaos reigned and change was in the air. Some Hungarians and Germans packed up their things and set off for their motherlands. One morning, on his way to the Village Hall to put together the news, Kalman spotted Kata Lorbach on a small but heavily laden caravan. He stopped and stared at her: she seemed deep in thought and somehow composed. Her eyes met his, and, after a moment of uncertain contemplation, she raised her hand to greet him. In spite of everything, Kalman felt touched by her gesture and, with equal uncertainty, returned the greeting. In all fairness, the scene did not so much fill him with sadness as give him a glimpse of the inconstancy of fate. In the Village Hall he found Béla and Mihály burning papers and stuffing others into suitcases. They paid little attention to him, too consumed by their own activities to give him more than a cursory glance. That day, his fresh autonomy in putting together the news was terminated, and he was presented with a brief and clear set of words:

Hear ye, hear ye!

Military authorities invite all loyal people of Bačka to place themselves in the service of the defense of the Hungarian homeland and all those who live there! All able-bodied men are called to report to the assembly point, Sokol House in Sombor, posthaste!
Notified!

That was the only news for the day, and Kalman made no objection to reading it. He finished the morning round—listless, desultory, and absentminded—and froze when a German mechanized convoy passed on the road in front of him; they were also pulling back and repositioning. That evening, the cell that had traveled with Matiša to Subotica met to stress the self-evident: the enemy was falling apart, and its forces were already in some kind of withdrawal; no one should lose their head, there was certainly more resistance to come, but the pieces on the chessboard of war were moving. German patrols were everywhere, and in ever greater numbers—that very day, one moved into a building at the boatyard! The final proposal was that all except Matiša pull back into the forest, a proposal spurred in part by the Hungarian announcement of mobilization. The same night, fifteen residents of Siga left for the forest. Kalman went with them, meaning his drum would not be heard in Siga for the foreseeable future.

By the next day, word reached the group in the forest that the police were pulling out of Siga, on foot, by way of the road toward Bezdan, with the exception of the one riding the bicycle, who followed behind, clumsily clutching his rifle and trying to shoot Toza. The dog relentlessly dodged the bullets, however. On the very first day in the forest, Kalman's group ran into Jakov Šomođvarac, who had also hidden among the trees with his stallion, which he loved more than anything else. Kalman begged to jump on his horse with him and try to catch up with the police and take back the bicycle. Šomođvarac reluctantly agreed, and soon they were riding through the village, giving chase like Furies. They caught up with the police right before the entrance to Bezdan, when they were already in range of the Bezdan sentries. They watched helplessly from a distance as the bicycle and Toza got farther and farther away. Later Šomođvarac would describe how Kalman at that moment did not once mention the bicycle, but fell to his knees and called through tears to Toza. The dog looked back briefly and then continued running after the bicycle and his canine fate. The officer had obviously at some point given up on shooting the dog—since Kalman and Šomođvarac did not witness any such attempt— but it is hard to say what kind of fate awaited him in the end. He never returned to Siga.

A smattering of people, mainly Hungarians, reported to the Sokol House, but most were unwilling, and a few hundred people, like Kalman's party, decided to withdraw into the forest.

True, they were there only to hide from possible mobilization, and many would return to their homes to spend the night, but in those days the forest was teeming with people. And they did not put that much effort into hiding; people nonchalantly walked into the forest with the confidence of true natives, occupying well-known spots without any great fear that someone would have a clue where to look for them. In fact, without any great worry that anyone would look for them at all. No one feared that any of the "loyal" population would point the police or the army in the direction of the forest.

Kalman's group was the only remotely armed one and reveled in its new wartime role. People competed over who would be the better soldier, with an advantage held by those who had served in the army before and had picked up certain skills. The biggest problem would prove to be a shortage of weapons.

Everyone wanted a rifle. And, as we know, there were only ten of them. Kalman took no part in these arguments, given that he was one of very few who had his own pistol and did not let it out of his sight. At the head of command, though without any particularly clear hierarchy or structure, was the quartet that had traveled to Subotica: Gubica, Marijanović, Pašić, and Škarica. Father Matiša occupied a special place in the organization, but he did not leave for the forest nor did he want to be overly involved in the part that involved arms. His realm was logistics. The group spent most of its time on the remote forest farm of Antun Kovač, with the occasional visit in moments of crisis to Franja Raič's cabin. With each passing day, their band grew bigger. Some of those who had taken temporary shelter in the forest had with time become frustrated with the circumstances they found themselves in—very quickly, in truth, after the first few days of forest life—so they joined Kalman's comrades, since they, armed and talking big, had clear intentions to resolve their frustrations. Hence new people constantly arrived, and with them the odd rifle. Soon, patrols were assigned to observe the roads and waterways around Siga. And that was how, on October 12, they caught sight of a column of Honvéd infantry, and behind them, at the very end of the column, eight Jews without any kind of special guard. The eight were being escorted from the Sombor airport via a bypass through Kupusina and along the riverbank toward Siga.

Ervin Vámoser, who only the previous day had retreated into the forest and evacuated his entire family from Klisa, had made his way to the Hunter's Lodge by the riverbank on the way to Kupusina in the hope he might find a rifle or two inside. It was an ideal spot from which to observe the riverbank. With him were two other men. They had no luck finding weapons, but they spotted the patrol and hid behind the crumbling wall of what was once a shed. The eight Jews stopped at the lodge to take a drink of water from the well. When Ervin saw that the Honvéd had moved on and were not looking back, he came out of his hiding place, approached the Jews, and invited them to flee and join them in the forest. They accepted. The next day, a patrol, which included Kalman, tasked to observe the road to Sombor, spotted a group of German soldiers driving about twenty Jews in front of them. At a bridge over the small Kiđoš River, the Germans forced the Jews into the water and sprayed them with bullets. Although Kalman and his comrades assumed there were no survivors, only after the war would they discover that was not the case. Endre Magyar from Kiskőrös survived the execution. Badly wounded, he somehow got himself to the river house of István Porsa, where the Kiđoš meets the Great Bačka Canal. Porsa found him a place to stay with the people of a nearby farm, who cared for him right up until October 22, the day Siga was liberated, when together with the eight Jews from the airport, he was taken to the hospital in Sombor. Later it was discovered that the poor man who had escaped execution was part of a larger group forced to work in the Bor copper mine. For a month they were driven to Vojvodina, where many met their fate: seven hundred at the brick factory in Crvenka and even more between Sivac and the Janjevo brick factory. For years after the war ended, people in Sombor would talk of the horrific treatment the Jews endured as they were driven through the town: one Bosnian Muslim soldier, holding a log with which he was bludgeoning his chosen victim, cried out: "Mujo, you hit him, I can't do it anymore!"

Kalman did not speak much during those days, not with the visible or the invisible, but instead, in a kind of paroxysmal state, went about his business in silence, gnashing his teeth. Never had his face worn such a look of seriousness. Comically so, since a person who is overly serious is hard to take seriously. There was the odd outburst of rage, when Kalman would become worked up out of all proportion over the smallest thing. Then he would hurl a few loud, angry words before silence was restored. The people around him gradually excluded him from decision-making. Not completely, since that could have caused problems, but they frequently presented him with decisions that had already been taken, dressing them up as self-evident, something it would be pointless to oppose. Kalman did not notice, or, if he did, owing to his general state of tension, he consented to everything respectfully served to him. Which altogether is not that hard, if on the other side you have someone who is so filled with fear, suffering so much that any lightening of the load comes as a blessing. For a man who finds himself in a situation in which, by his nature, he does not belong, and who for some or other reason of his own is living the life of someone else completely, it is important to satisfy form in order that he not fall apart at the seams. All the same, that October 20, Kalman was present at the crucial meeting and demonstrated his courage when many others did not. Perhaps not entirely of his own will, but still! After all, who knows who is in charge inside someone so taciturn?

IVAN VIDAK

The meeting was held after a large gathering at which almost no one expressed readiness to enter the fray. Although Kalman's forest band now numbered about a hundred people, to the proposal of a handful of the most agile that the liberation should begin without delay, only Kalman responded positively. This came as a fair surprise to many, though it was not the first time that Kalman had made a decision no one expected of him, since no one knew what kind of whip was driving him. In any case, everyone else was opposed, preferring to wait instead for the Russians. If they were close, what was the point in risking death? Are we really the kind of people to let others do our job for us? asked the incredulous initiators of the idea. And later that evening, a smaller meeting was held in Ampovo near Crna Bara. Around the fire sat Kalman, Ivica Pašić, Ervin Vámoser, and Stipan Kovač-Bentaroš. It was decided that at around midday the next day, they would move on the Village Hall and seize control. The police were no longer around. Only the guards remained, and they knew them, so it would be easier. At around midnight, they crossed the canal by rowboat at Krečana and spent the night at Kalman's. The next day at twelve, they walked into the middle of the road, armed with two rifles and Kalman's pistol (Vámoser did not manage to get ahold of a gun) and set off in the direction of the Village Hall. Those whom they met moved out of their way, like a Wild West showdown at high noon. It was fascinating how they ignored the guards in front of the Village Hall, and how the guards made no attempt to stop them. They entered without knocking and asked as to the whereabouts of Mihály Andrássy and clerk Béla. They were directed to a room in which was sitting a relative of Mihály, Valentin Andrássy, a young man barely twenty years of age who had recently been hounded out of his studies in Pest for bad behavior. He briefly informed them that the "real" Mihály and Béla had left the village and turned everything over to him. Kalman's group told the lad that their time was over and that he was also welcome to leave. Valentin did not resist; he turned over the keys to the cashier's office and the archive, and then Mihály Nikolin, the guards' commanding officer, signed a record to say that "on the twenty-first of October, nineteen forty-four, three military rifles, one light machine gun, two bayonets, six cartridge belts, and one hand grenade were turned over to Ivica Pašić." It is not known what happened to the rest of the weapons or when they got their hands on the light machine gun and the bombs. A small group of influential people quickly came together at the Village Hall, some after word reached them in the forest, others from their homes. They met, deliberated, and minutes were written. And it was precisely those minutes that became the first news delivered by Kalman after a short break, and the first since liberation:

Hear ye, hear ye!

Today, the 21st of October, Siga has been freed from enemy occupation! At a meeting in the Village Hall, the new authorities reached the following conclusions:

First!

Measures implemented to secure the village:

On the disarming of the former occupying guards, all arms have been gathered. The occupying guards have been dismissed; a guard composed of Slav volunteers of our village is to be formed.

Comrade Đipanov Antun is appointed guard commander, while to the post of controller over the execution of orders issued by the local National Liberation Committee is named comrade president Ivan Pašić, with comrades Živko Šomođvarac and Marin Pejak. Four permanent guard points have been designated: the first at the entrance to the village, with a force of four guards by day and two more by night; the second at the exit from the village from the northwest side, with a force of three permanent guards; third at the embankment at the edge of the young forest, at the destroyed bridge over the canal, as a night station of eight to twelve guards, since this point is at greatest risk, due to the many deserting Hungarian army Honvéd at the bridgehead crossing at Batina and potential enemy operations in our direction; and the fourth guard point, as a night station, where the fast Danube enters our little Danube. This is to secure the village, since, via forest patrols at Lower Siga, Šmaguc, and Kalandoš, it was found that around the Forest tavern there are Hungarian army patrols. This guard point is of six to eight men with a light machine gun, when they are not required at the third guard point.

Second!

Make preparations for:

The handover of cold weapons and firearms.

The closure of all hospitality objects and a ban on wine decanted in private homes.

The handover of military footwear, clothing, radio equipment; the removal of Hungarian signs from shops, streets, and offices; the designation of times when the civilian population can move about the village and outside of the village.

Third!

Besides the post office clerks, we are appointing three guard-tele-phonists on four-hour rotations to receive any eventual news as soon as the switchboard is working in Sombor. They are: Pavle Burgin, Stipan Šuvak, and Marin Vinkov.

In accordance with the first act of the Local National Liberation Committee, Ivan Pašić is considered president!

Notified!

In the process of taking over control, during the afternoon of October 21, there were several interesting developments in Siga. Ivan Pašić ordered that red stars be sown onto caps and eighteen Hungarian Honvéd surrendered, meaning the Local Committee got ahold of another eighteen rifles and other equipment and used them to arm the guards. The Honvéd had fled from Bezdan. They spent the night in Siga, where they surrendered, and were released the next day under permits to move around. After that they could go where they wanted. The forest ranger Marko "Lola" Ermenić detained two ss members when he stepped into the road with a rifle in his hands and stopped them on their motorbike. They didn't put up much of a fight. They were born in Prigrevica and were headed for Bezdan through Siga. Ervin Vámoser interrogated them. By the time the guards stopped a group of twelve Royalist Serbian national-ist guerillas known to clash with Tito's Partisans that afternoon who had decided to surrender, the newly installed authorities could hardly contain their jubilation and pride. Though con-trary to orders, that evening Kalman witnessed some serious drinking among his comrades in the Village Hall, where, how-ever, it was all so genuinely innocent and happy that he wanted to join in too. But he didn't, for reasons of his own. And even without those reasons, if Kalman had still been self-medicating with alcohol, it's possible he would have held himself back on that occasion, since Ivica Pašić had entrusted him with a particularly important task the next day. In the morning, after worshippers had left Mass, Kalman jumped up onto a large stone in the churchyard, banged his drum, and read out the following message:

Dear country folk,

Three years ago, a wave of fascism swept over us, over the whole of Europe. It did not spare our own country and challenged the Slavic colossus in the East. As a small people of the European community, we were threatened with complete destruction, or at the very least long years incapable of independent life. But fortune, comrades, did not smile on the fascists; the great Slavic peoples united, and together with their allies, the United States of America and Great Britain, stood as a bulwark against the further spread of fascist rule, and today are finishing the job of liquidating its last remnants. And the peoples of Yugoslavia played and still play today a visible role in that struggle for justice, freedom, and self-determination. Since a people that is not prepared to sacrifice lives for freedom is not worthy of that freedom. Marching side by side with our allies, we are today liberating the last corners of our homeland. We ourselves, you see, began our own liberation yesterday, and in freedom await our Slavic brothers, the glorious Red Army and the Partisan army with Comrade Tito at its head.

Accordingly, the National Liberation Committee in Siga yesterday took the administration and security of the village into its own hands, having disarmed the remaining fascists in our locality. Our aim, dear comrades, is to maintain order in the village, prevent reprisals, and secure the lives and property of us all, regardless of national affiliation.

Long live Yugoslav Marshal Josip Broz Tito! Long live the Red Army! Long live Marshal Stalin!

Kalman's speech was heard by about one hundred fifty people, who, when he finished, called out: "Long live comrade Tito! Long live freedom! Long live the Red Army!" Father Matiša was among them, but he merely applauded and did not shout. Kalman did not linger in the delighted crowd. There was too much else to do that day.

5.

ALREADY ON OCTOBER 22, the first Soviets appeared in Siga. Two arrived by motorbike, spoke briefly with a few curious locals, and returned to Sombor. Nikola "Toša" Depalov, the political commissar of the Sombor Partisan detachment, arrived four days later to make sure that everything was primed to establish a military post and to enroll new fighters. There was already much talk of large-scale military preparations on the Danube at Bezdan, on the other side of the river from the village of Batina. It was made clear that it would be good if Siga would send more fighters with the Twelfth Vojvodina Brigade and assist in the challenges that lay ahead. Some of Siga's young people had already joined the Partisans in previous years, but now more were needed. The brigade itself had been in position at Bezdan since October 29, but it was only at the beginning of November that its commanding officer, Borislav "Kuštra" Štrbački, stopped by, giving a speech with Ivica Pašić in the yard of the Village Hall before some three hundred residents of

Siga, Father Matiša among them. Afterward, some forty people joined the ranks of the Twelfth Vojvodina Brigade, Kalman the only one of prominence among them. Marijanović, Pašić, and Škarica all stayed to take care of newly liberated Siga. Although no one would have stopped them had they really wanted to go, it would be fair to say that the army required younger people who knew how to swim and row, people of the water. And Kalman, as we know, was exactly such an individual. Maybe not completely and maybe not always, but there was no doubt whatsoever that Kalman knew how to swim and to row, thanks to years spent on the water around the Tench. The storming of the Danube was being prepared, and the help of locals would be of great importance. It was with this in mind that they were seeking fighters. What Siga lacked in numbers it made up for in the special skills of its inhabitants. Kalman felt an unbridled sense of importance when he was entrusted with a number of crucial tasks to be carried out prior to battle.

But perhaps a word or two first about the battle that was being prepared. In their advance on Budapest, the Soviets had first headed south and, in liberating Belgrade, had liberated also a large part of Vojvodina, with the intention of crossing the Danube and continuing north to the Hungarian capital. That is how the Battle of Batina came about. By enlisting in the Twelfth Vojvodina Brigade, Kalman had reported to a strike unit, specially created for the occasion and which would be among the first to cross the Danube and form a bridgehead. An incredible doggedness and sense of purpose still raged within him. Experienced Communist Youth members, volunteer fighters, eyed this beginner with suspicion and were not particularly motivated to get to know him better. His reputation as a local familiar with the water opened doors he should not have passed through. He was very briefly trained in handling Soviet arms and then, with a few others, taken to the Siga boatyard to help prepare the vessels, as if he was a rower and a swimmer qualified too in the building and repair of boats. But that is often simply the way the army works, deploying the unskilled to positions of strategic importance. A fairly large number of small fishing boats were divided into two groups: those that would remain autonomous, and those that would be transformed into pontoon platforms by joining ten together and covering them with planks to create a motor-driven ferry. Kalman was proud to have been given such an important job. Though he had none of the expert knowledge expected of a boatyard worker, he put everything he had into preparing and repairing those vessels, acting as if he had the expertise and authority to such a degree that he soon spontaneously began taking charge. A symptom of his nervousness, no doubt, and very quickly the old and experienced workers complained to those who were actually in charge, and Kalman was returned to his unit. There he discovered that word had somehow reached his commanders about his work as town drummer, so he was given the job of courier. That was when the battle role assigned to him finally took shape: with the first group of fighters, in the main volunteers from all battalions of the Twelfth Vojvodina, he would cross the Danube, participate in establishing the bridgehead, and then, alone or with wounded soldiers, cross the river as and when necessary in order to maintain communication between the bridgehead and the command post on the other bank. As is often the way, an inexperienced individual is unaware of the scale of horror that awaits them, and so Kalman sensed only importance, honor, and status.

He spent the days leading up to the Battle of Batina wandering around Bezdan, jostling with rivers of people for provisions, watching cinema projections of Soviet war films, and, in essence, reveling in the crowded, chaotic, and loud interruption to reality. The only thing that really bothered him concerned a more familiar sphere of life: Would the role of Siga town drummer be assigned to someone else in his absence? But even that did not particularly perturb him, since who would dare try to trip him up so crudely? "No chance," he told the Voice. "Me? When I've done so much for the fight for freedom?" He felt stronger still because of the sea of soldiers in which he swam; all those Soviets, among them many Asian faces too, inspired awe, and he felt a warmth and comfort being part of them. That said, the excited clamor of a few days earlier had died down considerably, and everyone was unusually calm. All they were left to deal with was to clean their weapons and check their equipment. Two days earlier, reconnaissance teams of the Third Ukrainian Front and Twelfth Vojvodina had crossed the Danube, under cover of night and completely undetected, and had already exchanged fire on the flanks. Somewhere below Beli Manastir Ridge, rockets blazed, mortars thundered, and rifles clattered. It would die down for a bit, and then start up all over again. During the night between November 10 and 11, as a persistent rain battered everything in its path and Kalman, from an outlying clump of trees right up against the Danube, observed a unit of Soviet engineers send a thick artificial fog down the main current of the river, the order arrived for his unit to ready for departure. At about midnight, as the rain abated, roughly eighty men boarded twenty small fishing boats. A group of Soviets crossed the river under a barrage of enemy fire. But Kalman's group waited. No sooner had the rain completely stopped than a strong wind picked up, bending trees and creating waves that further eroded the bank. Officers visited the boats, gave speeches, and galvanized the men. But their lofty words about the political moment and history being written were lost on many of them, given their complete ignorance of such grandiose ideas and the tension that had by then seriously gnawed away at their nerves. At six o'clock sharp, they got the order to move. The sun had yet to rise. Had he not had to row, Kalman would have felt his hand clenching and muscles twitching. Perhaps he looked completely horrified, but no one could see it through the darkness and fog, for which he could not fathom whether it was real or made by the Russians. Due to the strength and speed of the current, their starting position was some fifty meters upstream from the place they were supposed to arrive at. They had to rely on the estimates of the local fishermen, since in such gloom it was impossible to take aim at anything. All they could see from the boats was the light from the blind lamp, closed at the front and so casting its light only toward those rowing behind the lead boat. The width of the Danube at that point was some five hundred meters, and the fighters who were squeezed into the boats had a long wait to reach the other bank. What would come first, the opposite bank or the German guns?

Suddenly, Kalman's boat thumped into muddy ground. Only then did he notice the other boats, some already aground, others just arriving. They carefully removed themselves from the vessels, gripped their rifles, and pulled grenades from their pockets. Kalman recalled the reconnaissance and knew that the first German trenches should be there, a few meters from the bank, right there where they had to disembark. All was calm and quiet, with the exception of the dull thud of battle being waged by the Soviets further to the north. But here, right by Batina itself, in the most fortified part, it was as if empty. A pale light was beginning to break through, the roofs of nearby houses discernible above the mist. The tension gripping Kalman eased by an almost imperceptible degree, enough for him to grab his canteen and tip water into his dry mouth, when a volley of bullets from a light machine gun ripped through the air above their heads. His comrades dropped to the ground around him. Someone grabbed him by the shoulder and yanked him down. "Grenades!" he shouted at Kalman. Kalman did as instructed, tossing two that exploded in the trenches and sprayed out bloody water that fell on them like rain. While he wiped the water from his face with the palms of his hands, his comrades wasted no time leaping into the trenches from which could now be heard a terrifying cacophony of sounds: rifle butts against helmets, the arrhythmic thump of steps, wailing, shots, the rattle of knives and bayonets. Kalman wanted to join them in the trench, but felt certain he could not. Realizing how much he did not belong in the strike unit of the Twelfth Vojvodina, wetness began to warm his groin. Covering his head with his hands, he thrust his sobbing face into the wet sand. "Why the silence?" he mumbled into the mud, painfully, barely audibly.

Moments later he sensed that the battle in the trench was losing force. Gritting his teeth, he wiped away his tears and began crawling to the edge, sniffing in the snot set loose by his crying. Peering down from the edge of the trench, he saw only the burly machine gunner, Toša, pounding the head of an ss soldier with the butt of a German rifle. The floor of the trench was strewn with bodies, mainly German. The other fighters had already jumped out of the trench and set off toward the center of Batina and the next line of defense, while others continued down the length of the trench, mopping up. Toša noticed the unfortunate Kalman when the German artillery began mercilessly pounding their position, whipping up a veritable shitstorm around them. He grabbed Kalman by his overcoat, pulled him into the trench, and ran off in search of where the battle was fiercest. Kalman stayed behind, sitting in the blood-drenched trench while the storm of artillery blazed above him. The Voice was gone, silenced completely. But at that moment Kalman felt no relief. What's more, he felt more alone than ever. "Why the silence?" he said, this time loud and clear. But nothing. Inside there was a deathly silence. Unable to contain himself anymore, Kalman began weeping uncontrollably. He dropped his rifle, slumped against the mud wall of the trench, and cried like never before, recognizing all his wretchedness beneath the storm of explosions that thundered above him. At that moment, a few steps from him, one of the Germans lying on the ground in the trench began pulling himself up, clearly wounded and dazed by the blast, but with the will to continue fighting. He gasped for breath and stumbled, struggling to get to his feet, but when he spotted before him the tearful Kalman he turned all his attention on him. In rage and panic the German found a rifle, reloaded, and pointed it at Kalman before Kalman had even grasped what was going on. Every living thing has a secret store of strength and determination for self-preservation, and hence how Kalman too reached for his rifle. But in the time it took him to pick it up, a bullet struck him in the left side of his gut. He squealed like an animal when the savage pain began pulsing through him, transforming in the blink of an eye into a slobbering attack of rage. Kalman's own shot found the German's face before he could fire off a second, settling everything without aim or intention and throwing the German on his back, bent at the knees. All the same, Kalman fired into him every bullet he had left in the Mosin rifle. Only when he had laid the hot barrel in the mud did he clutch painfully at the wound from which warm blood quietly flowed. Due to the sheer amount of snot running from his nose, he was forced to breathe through his mouth, which had now become painfully dry. "Why the silence? I need to know! Why are you not talking, you fucking fuck?" he cried, so hard that the weeping of a moment earlier seemed like a distant memory. He grabbed at his hair and screamed. The screams he let out over the following few minutes were in the worst possible taste; we can say more about them by not getting into their description at all. But they too came to an end, as did all that unbridled rage. Kalman passed out, though at that moment it felt to him like he was slipping into a life-saving, peaceful sleep.

First he heard what sounded like a drumroll. Then he recoiled from an intolerable stench in his nose. "Molodec," said a satisfied Mariya Ivanovna Lomonosov, stroking his face. He was still in the trench. The early autumn darkness had already descended, shooting and explosions reverberated all around, and the sky was lit up by flares, one after another. But the pretty face of the Soviet doctor (medical student, to be precise) filled his field of vision. She bandaged his wound with dedication and determination and called out to Messrs Alyosha and Taras, two strapping men who dragged Kalman out of the trench, placed him on a stretcher, and, stooping, carried him to the riverbank. There were many wounded around him, some groaning, calling out for their families. But Kalman, pale and morbidly composed, kept silent. There were both Partisans and Red Army men there now, the battle having mixed them all up by the evening. At some point the face of Mariya appeared once more at his side, this time offering him a drink of water from a tin canteen. "Nu, batyushka," she said to him, and continued giving water to the wounded. Kalman turned and looked for the face of this woman, haunted by it as something almost inappropriately beautiful for the circumstances in which he found himself. At that moment, hands grabbed his stretcher once more, and he was carried onto the deck of a small, sturdy tugboat called *Old Bečej*, which, even without the name clearly written on its side, Kalman would have recognized from the Siga boatyard. Attached to the tug with steel cables were two metal platforms that, like the deck of the tug, were now covered with wounded men. German artillery pounded the Danube relentlessly. Shells fell all around, throwing up geysers of water as if the river was boiling. The *Old Bečej* was very soon overloaded with wounded and set off for the Vojvodina bank across the boiling waters that washed over onto the deck and furiously rocked the boat. The terror increased with each flare that illuminated the dramatic opera playing out on the river, and the screams of the wounded grew more intense. It would have been easier in the dark. Kalman did not scream. He gave no sign of anxiety whatsoever. He lay calmly on the stormy deck and observed the blazing sky, the smoke carried quickly on the wind, and breathed in the drops of water, big and small, that splashed the deck. He averted his gaze only to look at Mariya each time she passed. The silence inside him was so deafening, so marked by the disappearance of the Voice, that no sound from the outside world could disturb it. If silence had ever made itself a throne, then that day it was in Kalman's head. At one moment, a cannon round struck the first platform tied to the boat and broke it in two. All of the wounded who were on it ended up under the dark, muddy surface of the water. Two managed to grab ahold of one of the tree trunks that for days had been riding the river. They did not cry out or panic, just mutely watched the tugboat as the current carried the trunk relentlessly into the darkness. Almost immediately a mortar round hit the sturdy tugboat at the tip of the bow and rocked it savagely. Mariya, who had been milling around nearby, was thrown several meters by the explosion, as a result of which she gave a brief cry and collapsed on the deck. That was the only other thing that Kalman recalled from the voyage: how one sharp sting tore him from the morbid calm in which he had been floating—the suffering of the woman whose hands had so gently pulled him from the darkness. With a jerk, he pulled himself up onto his hands, but because of the movement his own wound sent such bolts of pain through him that, weak as he was, he slipped once more into the darkness of unconsciousness.

He awoke thirty-six hours later in Sombor hospital. The Battle of Batina was still being waged. Through the window, however, he glimpsed a perfectly sunny and peaceful day. Everything hurt and he was weak, able only to lift his head a little. "Good morning, fighter," said a voice from the next bed. It was the machine gunner, Toša, who had pulled him into the trench that morning after disembarking. From their brief conversation, he discovered that the second wave that day had begun only at four in the afternoon. By that point his unit had been all but decimated, but they had managed to hold their positions. Even Kalman understood that it was a miracle he had not bled to death lying in that mud all day. "And the doctor?" Kalman asked Toša, who of course knew nothing about her. At the moment Kalman was being extracted, Toša was still shooting. And she was only one of many aiding the wounded.

A nurse soon appeared, then a doctor. They gave Kalman water, asked whether he was in pain, gave him medicine. He was told he had been lucky, that the bullet had passed through him without causing much damage, and that was why he had not bled to death. Forty days' recovery, and everything would be fine. Good news indeed. Kalman could stop worrying about his health and devote his attention to the more important questions that, if not tormented him, certainly occupied him: What had happened to the Voice? Where had the Voice disappeared to and, more important, would he come back? He could at least hazard a guess. Had the Voice become scared because he had no answer? In all likelihood, that prattling sage, that interfering know-it-all, had nothing to say in that muck-filled trench. What a humiliation! What a demise! Although he had no sure answer, the sound of

Kalman sniggering to himself echoed through the hospital the whole afternoon. They had to ask him to stop.

He spent the following weeks exclusively in the immovable silence of his mind. In the bloody river in which those hospital beds floated, he quickly understood his privileged position: one of very few with his head above the water. And no one else in those unfortunate circumstances felt like a man who, at the very moment an earthquake razed his home, found out he had just won millions in the lottery. And that golden silence he listened to so attentively, like Buddha achieving enlightenment, resembled a warm, healing spa in which his body was laid, high above the bloody river in which these unfortunate wretches around him floated. His limp hands, no longer clenched, rested mutely at his side. He heard every rustle of the sheet beneath his little finger. In the end, he could swear he also heard the gentle cracking of his nails as they grew—it was that quiet.

"Comrade, in a few days' time you can try and take a short walk," Doctor Čičovački told him after a few weeks, worried about Kalman's apparently listless state. "It's nothing to be ashamed of, you know. Depression is to be expected."

Kalman gave a small smile and said, "It's okay doctor, no problem. I'll take a walk."

And true enough, he did walk those days. After all, why wouldn't he? Already on his first walk he came to the conclusion that, despite the cold, going out into the yard was the only thing that made any sense; hospital corridors, not to mention rooms, were best avoided. Not that he had not already become numb to his new surroundings. Over the past few weeks, many in the neighboring beds had moved to the grave in indescribable suffering. But nevertheless, why suffer the conditions in the hospital more than necessary? Then he met a man from Siga, eighteen-year-old Ivica Patarić, a carpenter wounded the same day as Kalman, albeit a little later, since he had been in the evening wave. Shrapnel had torn a piece of flesh from his shoulder, but it would be okay. They exchanged a few words, Ivica asked for a cigarette, but Kalman did not smoke. He asked the young carpenter whether he had been bandaged and cared for by that young Russian doctor, but he hadn't. Ivica was cared for by a Partisan medic. In spite of the warm ocean of divine silence, Kalman's thoughts often turned to Mariya Ivanovna Lomonosov, though he did not even know her name. More and more her gentle face would enter his mind's eye, especially now when he had recovered a little, woken from his reverie, and started to walk. He recalled her soft hand on his cheek after that stench had awakened him from the dead. The hand smelled of soap; how was that possible? But then some kind of commotion would snap him out of his thoughts, someone shouting, playing cards, cracking a joke or arguing, and slowly but surely he would be dragged back into life's trivial tick tock. Nights and mornings would be reserved for smiles in the ocean of silence, and daytime for conversation, walking, and concern over how to get ahold of a decent bite of food. He asked the doctors and the wounded Soviets whether they perhaps knew the young woman, but they all shrugged their shoulders blankly. And the face of Mariya began to blur in his mind and became harder and harder to retrieve. Soon he was visited by a delegation from Siga. Completely by chance, comrades Pašić and Škarica heard that he was in Sombor hospital and one Sunday set off to see him. The Battle of Batina had ended, and everyone was feeling more at ease. Pašić and Škarica told him that the Party had appointed new leadership in Siga, people who for some reason suited it more.

"Imagine, turns out they're more deserving than us!" Škarica howled, half-joking.

They had not been completely forgotten, however, since they were nevertheless given positions of responsibility. Pašić, for example, managed the hemp-spinning mill, while Škarica oversaw the boatyard in which they were now fixing up the vessels damaged in the battle. The *Old Bečej*, it seemed, would also survive, along with its captain, Matija Galić. The tugboat's name once again conjured for Kalman the ineffable face of his savior, and he told them of his wounding and the young female doctor to whom he would forever be indebted, whose name he did not know, nor whether she was still among the living.

"Well, did you go to fight or to chase skirts?" the sniggering pair ribbed him.

Though it was all innocent, Kalman regretted having said anything and immediately changed the subject by asking what was new in Siga. If he meant his job, they said, he should know that a temporary replacement had been found, but he should have no fear for his job. They gave him a guarantee. After all, who would drive him, a wounded fighter, from his place of work? The guarantee was of great importance to Kalman, since he considered his job practically an organic extension of himself. Satisfied, he drummed his hands on the bare table at which they were sitting, only to be halted quickly by a warning from the wound in his gut.

"Enjoy this big bird," Pašić said, placing a roast chicken in front of him. "Who knows when you'll get the chance again."

The people of Siga had slaughtered much livestock and poultry, transporting to the battlefield six wagons of meat. They would not easily make up for it under these conditions. But nor should they worry; they were not starving yet. In Siga, there was always enough to go around. They also brought him a bottle of mulberry rakija, in case the front line had returned him to drink (would anyone hold it against him?). But it hadn't. Alcohol hadn't even crossed his mind.

Not long after, Kalman was told he would be released from the hospital on Christmas Eve. With only a few days to go, he decided to offer the bottle of mulberry rakija to a few of the wounded in the neighboring beds. Toša had been moved, but there were others who gladly accepted the offer. Obviously, they had to go out into the yard and drink in secret. Kalman joined them for the company.

"Pour it quicker, before he changes his mind," said Ilija from Veliki Bečkerek, who was the main source of amusement, since both his arms were in plaster and the others had to pour the spirit into his mouth.

It was a particularly joyful moment, full of happiness for people who were in need of some. Everything was white, and the snow was still falling. And then he saw her, on the other side of the yard, on a narrow, concrete path swept of snow, her right leg missing below the knee. She was practicing walking with crutches. Although it had seemed to Kalman that he could no longer recall her face, recognition was instantaneous, unstoppable, carried on a powerful wave of adrenaline. He could see her face, which was turned toward him, and there could be no doubt. It was as if it was illuminated by a different light. An inexplicable delight took hold of him, he even asked himself, "Why, for God's sake, did I get so hung up on that doctor?" But he made no effort whatsoever to come up with an answer. He left his comrades in arms with some unconvincing explanation, but, busy pouring each other drinks, they paid no attention. He began walking toward her. Only then did he notice her other physical characteristics: she was relatively short, shorter than him, of stout build and wide hips, but well proportioned. Like Kata Lorbach, only shorter and more beautiful. With little strength in her hands, the way in which she struggled with the crutches suggested tenderness, a femininity that was practically graceful. He stopped a few steps short of her. That's when she looked at him for the first time and revealed her large green eyes. Brown hair, greasy, tied in a ponytail. "How come I didn't remember the color of her eyes?" thought Kalman.

He said hello. She said hello back. He offered to help, and then the language barrier reared up between them. Kalman began at great length, using his arms and legs, and she shrugged, understanding the odd fragment when the gestures, a string of words she recognized, and his facial expressions would come together in the correct constellation. She understood that Kalman was suggesting they sit on the bench nearby, but given that it was covered in snow, she proposed they sit somewhere inside. She was not reserved or intimidated but bright and extroverted, friendly. Amazing. She showed no fear at all of men she did not know. Perhaps it was the influence of the army. Kalman accepted her suggestion, and they quickly found a seat in the warm. Our people do not immediately understand Russian. But all Slavic peoples have the good fortune that they can nevertheless, by listening carefully and actively, identify words that are similar. And the longer and more attentively we listen, the secret of that other Slavic language starts to unravel before us, and, more and more, with greater and greater certainty, we are illuminated by the light of understanding. And that is how these two understood one another: Serbo-Croatian versus Russian. First they exchanged names, as is customary. And then Kalman began to explain who he was and how he knew her.

"Molodec," Mariya said, laughing loudly and showing beautiful white teeth.

"Yes, yes, I'm molodec!" he said, remembering the word even though, till that moment, he would not have known to repeat it.

She could have found it abhorrent, she could have found it boring to make small talk with some Partisan, one of the thousands of fighters whose aid she had come to over the past three years, one of the thousands she was now surrounded by. But she didn't. And she herself was surprised by the easy impression Kalman had left on her. She was twenty-three years old and had been in the second year of medical school when the war began. She was born in Vladivostok, where she still lived with her mother and older sister. Her father had died in an accident at sea. Immediately in the summer of 1941, she had volunteered as a nurse in the Red Army. Only last year, on its establishment, she found herself part of the Third Ukrainian Front, and her path took her to Batina. She had seen plenty, but this was the first time she had been wounded, and, unfortunately, rather seriously: left without the lower part of her right leg because the bone had been crushed beyond repair. Speaking about her predicament, her mood turned, which, to his own surprise, Kalman found most upsetting.

"Ah, that's nothing," he said, waving his hand so convincingly that he managed to raise even his own spirits. "Mechanization today is developing so fast that soon we won't even need legs."

She didn't understand a word, but she felt his cheerfulness and smiled. Then she began questioning Kalman about this and that, at first generally and then in greater and greater detail. She very much liked the fact that Kalman was a town drummer. And Kalman tried so hard to understand her questions as well as possible, tried so hard to enter her head that he somehow succeeded, after an eternity, to drive a small spark of life back into his genitals. It was not about anything so vulgar as an erection, but a kind of vibration, an impulse, electricity. He felt ashamed. He blocked out and hid this newly awakened passion like a family disgrace that is ignored but is impossible to escape. The effort generated yet another dose of energy, an impulse, a focus on her. And so toward the end of that first, hours-long interaction, he began to discreetly, awkwardly, and briefly touch her hands, tap her on the shoulder—anything to feel the warmth of her skin. Mariya did not object. She saw nothing inappropriate in it, since she found Kalman, above all, infinitely naive, and so did not consider him a threat. She did not see in him any kind of calculation, any kind of plan or ill intent. She liked his nervousness. Of late, there was little that had the power to turn her thoughts from her lost leg and the existential torment on the horizon, despite the fact she tried to be cheerful and friendly. Déformation professionnelle, perhaps. The last thing she was expecting was the affection of some boy, even if only a local peasant who knew little about the world beyond his parish. They parted warmly, happily, both of them beaming from ear to ear, but they did not plan any future meeting. They hurried along because it was dinnertime, and food then had a different value than in peacetime. So without much reflection, they warmly wished each other goodbye, shook hands so as to touch one another, Kalman at least, and set off to their rooms smiling.

Kalman savored his soup and potatoes that evening like never before. But soon after dinner, when his enthusiasm had worn off a little, he found himself in great torment. How would he find her again tomorrow, when it had taken them more than a month to meet the first time? Kalman had walked the length and breadth of the hospital before, more or less aware that he was indeed looking for her, and not once did he find her. Perhaps it would be easier now that he knew her name. Hand on heart, he had not really searched for her before. In reality, he had walked around the hospital in the hope that he might come across her, if she was alive. There is a difference. He hadn't met anyone then who would have recognized her, who had been on the *Old Bečej* at the same time as him. He had already started thinking that it had been a mirage and that he was suffering from some new sickness, now that the Voice was no longer around. But, really, how would he find her tomorrow? He wrestled with the worry in bed, tossing and turning, and each time he thought that sleep was getting the better of him, he had the urge to pee. Round and round like that, right up until almost dawn, when he finally passed out for a few hours. Who would have thought he would so quickly build up tolerance of the new silence inside him?

In the morning, Kalman observed the hangovers afflicting his rakija-soaked comrades. It was a sorry sight. "Did I really live like that?" he thought. He got up and ate a plate of polenta that they had brought in. He ate quickly, but without the delectation of the night before, and hurried outside into the snow-covered yard. On the way he heard a large, mustachioed commander loudly addressing a unit of wounded men gathered around him: "Comrades, peace is the most beautiful woman. Not everyone can have her!" His attention grabbed, Kalman stopped for a second and started thinking, before he snapped himself out of it and resumed the search. Perhaps not simply a happy coincidence but, somehow, the collusion of two wills, Kalman's misery was quickly cut short when he found Mariya at the same spot where he had set eyes on her the day before. No one had managed yet to clean the path of snow from the night before, so her crutches were slipping and she could barely stay upright. Without even approaching her or saying hello, Kalman raced to the storehouse and took a wide wooden snow shovel and a broom. At the door stood several buckets of ash from the stove, so he grabbed one and headed back to Mariya. She was evidently pleased to see him, smiling warmly, but Kalman did not blink an eye; there was no time for frivolous courtesy. Instead, he swiftly set to work with the shovel, clearing the snow from the path. Immediately his wound began to hurt, so he slowed his pace and began working with just one arm. Mariya stood to one side, a discreet smile of satisfaction spreading across her face. Her hair was down; she had somehow managed to wash it

IVAN VIDAK

since last they'd seen one another. Kalman cleared the worst of the snow with the shovel, then took hold of the broom for a finer clean before he spread the crumbling ash over the thin, frozen layer that was left.

"Comrade Mariya Ivanovna Lomonosov, your path!" he said grandiosely.

Mariya clapped her hands delightedly, balancing awkwardly on her crutches, and called out: "Kalman, a true gentleman you are!"

Then they took up their positions without any prior arrangement: Mariya on her freshly prepared path and Kalman standing to the side, watching attentively. Something powerful inside them galloped ahead of reason, pulling them forward into a region cloaked in the shade of future events, where nothing could be seen but from which it was practically impossible to flee; a dazzling and utterly uncertain promise of the future stared into them as much as they stared into it. Understandably, that whole charade around the crutches did not last long; neither of them had the patience for it, so they quickly found a comfortable and secluded corner of the hospital, where they stayed all day, even foregoing lunch. They talked, waving their arms, drawing in the air and on the floor, anything in order to understand one another better. As the day wore on, the more they were joined by some illuminated intimacy, a bridge across which they could travel between one another. Dinnertime found them sitting in the same spot, tired and all talked out. A silence suddenly took over, a tense intermediate state, an emptiness between two points in time that provided an excellent occasion for Kalman to announce that he would be leaving the hospital in two days' time. Mariya froze. As if surrendering to events, she wished him a swift recovery at home, told him to take care and that she was sure the war would soon be over. And, who knows, perhaps they would meet again one day. Her words pained Kalman, as if she was genuinely saying goodbye. But how, after everything? Did he read something wrong? He asked how much longer she would have to remain in the hospital and what her plans were afterward. She replied that her wound had closed but that a good deal more time was needed for it to really, properly heal. And that she would probably be sent home soon to Russia. That was when Kalman decided enough was enough, and he openly invited her to join him in Siga. Why could she not convalesce there?

"Kalman, that's impossible," Mariya replied.

"Why?" Kalman asked her determinedly, adding that they were companions from the war, comrades in arms, who could stop them?

Kalman noticed how taken Mariya was by his initiative and resolve, awakening once more that passion, that electricity within him. Feeling as if he might faint from fear, that his heart would leap out through his throat, he seized the moment—it was now or never—and took hold of her hand, his gaze directed at the ground. He lifted his eyes when he felt that she had not pulled her arm away and, in fact, was squeezing his hand, which until that moment had been limp. His whole body was imbued with a fine tremor, shot through with an unbearable tension that briefly halted when she spoke.

With utter seriousness, Mariya said, "Kalman, you are aware that I have only one leg? You know, the other one won't grow back."

There was no sadness in her words; they radiated strength and acceptance. Instead of giving an answer, Kalman was again gripped by the tremor, the tension and passion. He leaned toward her and, with dry, trembling lips, tenderly kissed her cheek. Mariya blushed, but her face grew serious. Silence and the sound of their breathing echoed along the hospital corridors. Everyone was either in the canteen or eating dinner in their rooms. Outside it was already pitch black. Mariya was the first to stand and, with the help of her crutches, took a few steps toward the door that stood next to them, at the end of the ground-floor corridor. She opened the door, looked at Kalman, and went through. Kalman glanced around, all aflutter, and then he too hurried through the door and closed it behind him. Mariya laid down her crutches and threw her arms around his neck, kissing him impatiently. Kalman, equally awkward, responded in kind, and they began biting, licking, and gasping. A moment later, at Mariya's initiative, they were on the cold concrete floor of the small storeroom, clutching so tightly it was as if they wanted to squeeze into one another. Clearly neither scared nor inexperienced, Mariya flipped Kalman onto his back, straddled him and, in a flash, skillfully maneuvered him inside her. It was wonderful, completely different for Kalman than ever before. There was no shame, no feeling of unwanted necessity, of coldly carrying out the commands of the body. And most important, there was no Voice. He looked at her white face, the blotches of natural blush on her cheeks, a few sweaty locks pasted to her temples, her nostrils, and slightly open mouth, in which he glimpsed rows of teeth.

"Wonderful. Wonderful," Kalman gasped, holding up the stump of her leg with his left hand so that it didn't rub on the cold floor.

And then it happened again: he climaxed and felt how Mariya's body began to quiver as if plugged into the electric grid. The next moment, her entire body clenched as she let out a scream and lit up the room like a bolt of lightning. Already worried, Kalman became paralyzed with fear. A bare bulb on the ceiling dimmed for a moment before sheepishly sputtering back to life. Mariya giggled ecstatically and lay down on top of him, her hair over his face and her warm breath on his neck. Once more she smelled entirely of soap. But then she stood up, looking for her crutches and fixing the nightgown she had on under a thick Soviet army coat. Lying on the floor, Kalman continued watching her rapturously and was shocked when he realized the next moment that she was weeping bitterly. He lifted himself up onto his elbows and tenderly spoke her name, to which she simply held out her hand, as if to stop him, and left the storeroom as fast as she could. Kalman quickly yanked his pajamas up from around his knees, wrapped himself in his coat, and went out after her into the corridor, but she was making great haste on her crutches, and the corridors were already beginning to bustle with people who had finished their dinner. He dared not make a scene. Worn out and dejected, he returned to his room, pulled the bedcovers over his head, and tried in vain to fall asleep.

The next morning, however, to his surprise he had little difficulty finding Mariya: she was waiting for him again at the concrete path in the hospital courtyard. It was a bright, sunny day, everything glittering from the snow. She approached and, without a word, gently rested her head on his shoulder. He embraced her. They spent the whole morning in sickly sweet and unrealistic conversation full of fantasies, as is often the way with young love. She asked him about Siga and what life was like there. Kalman weaved together a story, adding and omitting where necessary, remaking his home for her.

"I will. I'll come with you to Siga," Mariya said in the end. "If they let us."

As if given a signal, they burst into action! Something opened up inside them; the floodgates lifted, and suddenly happiness and hope were in abundance. They agreed that the first step should be for each of them to inform their superiors of their intentions and to seek permission, since both of them were still members of the army, which had its own rules. Kalman's situation was perhaps a little easier, since he was not out in the big wide world, far from home, and not a woman, in the army no less. First, they told the senior ranks of the hospital, Yugoslav and Soviet, who then passed on the information to the commanders of the units to which Kalman and Mariya officially belonged. The very next day, the day before Kalman was due to be discharged from the hospital, delegations of both armies arrived. Kalman's lot were more than happy with the idea. For them, it was like some living testament to their joint effort, a monument to the Battle of Batina, of great rhetorical and propaganda value. They slapped him on the back, offered him rakija, asked if there was anything he needed, as if they were family and friends who had come to celebrate his engagement.

"Are you going to marry her?" asked a burly captain.

"If she'll have me, comrade captain," Kalman answered crisply.

The Soviets, however, were more serious, more cautious. They questioned Mariya exhaustively, wanting to know all the circumstances, and not one question did they consider too inappropriate to ask. It was decided on the Soviet side that a commission would be formed to consider the case in detail and issue its verdict. Mariya explained to them that Kalman was leaving the hospital the next day and that she would like it— "Obviously, comrade, if at all possible"—if the decision of the commission would not be unnecessarily long in coming.

"All in good time, comrade, all in good time," the earnest Soviets told her, as if immersed in a game of cards.

That evening, Kalman and Mariya felt trapped in a kind of limbo, although there was still hope. At that moment the greatest torment was the fact that Kalman would be discharged the next day, while she still knew nothing and was unable to leave the hospital. They sat on a bench and cuddled openly; they did not care, and many already knew what was going on and were entertained by it. They no longer went to the storeroom, however. It seemed to them inappropriate to indulge in sex at such a moment, when so much was at stake, although it was something that went unspoken. They simply understood one another. And it would have been difficult to hide themselves away somewhere, now that they were a well-known hospital couple.

　　　　　　　　IVAN VIDAK

That same evening, Kalman was called to the hospital office, because someone was trying to reach him by phone. Walking to the office, he feared that his superiors had changed their mind. After all, there was a war going on, and there was not much room or understanding for extravagances like theirs. On the other end of the line, however, was General Kosta Nagy himself, the chief Partisan commander at Batina. He said he had been told everything and that it was a splendid thing that Kalman was doing, important for the friendship of these brotherly nations, and that he had spoken personally to Marshal Fyodor Tolbukhin and that there would be no problem. Of course, the commission would do its job, those were the rules, but the request would be granted. And he should feel free to tell his sweetheart, to put her mind at ease too. Like an excited child clutching the receiver with both hands, Kalman was so gushing in his thanks that the general had to put the phone down. Mariya was pleased too, but did not get carried away, since life had taught her to fear sudden surprises.

Kalman reassured her soothingly, "He's a general, by God! He wouldn't just say it."

The only issue that remained, Kalman was sure, was his discharge the next day, and who could say when her commission would sit. But the next morning, as Kalman reluctantly prepared to leave, the news arrived that the commission would meet the following day at the hospital. While she still harbored some doubts, for Kalman it was a forgone conclusion. He would go home and return for her the next day. Even better, since it gave him time to ready and clean the house for her arrival. After their reluctant parting, Kalman sat in the jeep that Ivica

Pašić had sent from Siga to pick him up, and which during the war had been at the disposal of the hemp mill that Pašić took care of. First they stopped by the Village Hall, where Kalman warmly greeted everyone. Stipan "Bell Ringer" Marijanović was still president of the Local National Liberation Board. His comrades in the Party had not sidelined him after all. But all the other faces were new. Straightaway, Kalman was introduced to the young Janik Francuz, a farm boy who had lost his parents and who was now doing Kalman's job.

"Please, come back to work as soon as possible. This guy's going to drive me crazy," Marijanović said of Francuz, who had been assigned the job of town drummer practically against his will. That is, he was put in the post so he would have enough to get by. But he complained endlessly that he wanted to return to the farm, because that was where his heart was and it was all he knew. Kalman calmly shook Francuz's hand, satisfied that the boy had no real designs on his job. After greeting all those gathered, Kalman called Marijanović to one side and explained discreetly that he would be bringing home a woman the next day, and that he had not a penny to his name.

"Of course, of course. I'd thought of that," said Marijanović. "You're owed two wages that you didn't get when you weren't here, all in order."

He pushed into Kalman's hand an envelope full of crisp banknotes. Kalman thanked him kindly, returned to the jeep, and headed home.

Everything was as he had left it: a mess. He had never cleared up the disarray that he and his comrades had left the house in when they spent the night there before their armed descent on

IVAN VIDAK

the Village Hall. Kalman set about clearing up. He returned everything to its rightful place, carefully and slowly, because he still felt his wound, but resolutely and untiringly. In the afternoon he returned to the Village Hall, asking to buy a little lime and some wood to burn. Marijanović said someone would bring it to him in an hour or two from the Hall's store. He needn't pay anything, since he'd already paid enough. But he should wait a second, given he was already there, and from another room Marijanović wheeled out a bicycle. Kalman's face lit up, though the thought of Toza quickly left him tight in the chest. He swiftly banished such thoughts and thanked Marijanović with a wide, satisfied smile. Clearly it was not the same bicycle. It was not even new. But it was in good condition, tuned and oiled, and it went like fury. Kalman rode it home along the frozen, ash-covered streets and continued working. When a small Soviet truck arrived a few hours later, laden with chopped wood and a sack of lime, all that remained was for him to stir the lime and refresh the old layer on the floors of the house. Lads from the Village Hall unloaded the wood and stacked it in the shed. They helped with the lime too. All in all they treated Kalman with great respect. He fell asleep still in his clothes, but tired and satisfied, so when the jeep's horn woke him in the morning, he simply leapt up, grabbed his coat from the chair, and headed outside. Arriving at the hospital in Sombor, he discovered that the Soviet commission was already sitting, and Mariya was with them in the office of the hospital manager. Kalman had little choice but to wait in the entranceway, hopping about nervously. Half an hour later, everything was decided. First to pass him was the grim-faced and grave Soviet commission, before he caught sight of two medics helping a smiling Mariya down the staircase. Kalman met her on the last step and took her in his arms. Ten minutes later they were sitting on the backseat of the jeep and traveling toward Siga. It was cold, and they were wrapped in their army coats, Mariya gripping tightly to the lapel, chilled to the bone, while Kalman had one arm around her shoulders and the other he enthusiastically pointed left and right at the winter landscape of the Siga district.

IVAN VIDAK

6.

KALMAN AND MARIYA saw in New Year 1945 completely alone. No doubt intentionally. They were invited here and there, told they were welcome everywhere—if for no other reason than curiosity—but they resolved to stay in. From the Village Hall they received a nice piece of venison. Now, when there was not enough livestock, hunters came in handy. Kalman cooked it as best he could, but it was completely unimportant, given that the only hunger they felt was of that other kind. And now, finally, the electric potential within Kalman showed itself in all its glory. If until recently he had felt inhibited by the Voice, now nothing stood in his way: Kalman Gubica and Mariya Ivanovna Lomonosov could not keep their hands off one another. In the beginning, they expected a repeat of what happened in the hospital storeroom, what Kalman was already familiar with from before: a flash of light, a strong spasm, and a bolt of astonishing energy bursting from Kalman's groin and coursing through his partner with ruthless force. That all happened again, but it was only the start. Repeating the ecstasy over and over again, the whole thing grew stronger and stronger, gaining in intensity, becoming increasingly explosive, to the degree that they no longer tried to explain it to themselves. Never, not at one moment, did either of them utter a word about what they were experiencing, about the orgasm inside which, and from which, they were living. It looked like this: after the first few times they had sex, with that familiar flash and electric orgasm, their room began to be filled with a warm, milky yellow light. It grew around them like a huge, illuminated yellow egg that first enveloped only them, like some kind of protective membrane, and then, through repetition of the act, expanded to the whole room. That milky yellow light, like all other elements of Kalman's electric orgasm, acted only on her. Kalman's own orgasm was of this world, most ordinary (is that not enough?), while all the power and wonder were for her. So when that yellow light would fill the room, Kalman would lie contented on the bed by the stove while Mariya, eyes closed and wearing the most satisfied smile Kalman had ever seen, would hover just beneath the ceiling, her arms, leg, and stump floating at her side as if in a state of weightlessness, as if in water. In that milky yellow light there were no worries, there was no tomorrow, as if they were immersed in yellow ataraxia, sustained by manna, in a state in which even words were no longer necessary. Every evening after sex, Kalman would lie on the bed and watch the miraculous floating of Mariya. He could not take his eyes off her, while she would only occasionally open hers and gaze down at him with a tender smile. At some point they would fall asleep, and by the time Kalman would wake at dawn, everything would be back to normal; only Mariya would be asleep somewhere on the floor, wherever the light had set her down. But it did not leave her, since she would still have around her that thin, yellow membrane of illumination. Then Kalman would pick her up and put her on the bed. He would leave for work, and when Mariya would wake, and that protective membrane disappeared, the world would once more look perfectly familiar and normal. There was no tough awakening, no hangover, so to say, only a gentle peace filled with satisfaction, when a person begins the day with their spirit wholly renewed.

Immediately, the first day of the new year, Kalman requested to return to work. He still felt his wound a little, but refused to let it stop him from continuing his work. His replacement was more than happy to oblige, so Kalman took back his drum and, full of appetite, set off for the first of his twelve crossroads.

Hear ye, hear ye!

Friendly Bulgarian forces arrive in Sombor! They will join the fight for the final liberation of all peoples and nationalities of our country!

János Tomajek, head of the estate of Rudolf Rosenberg, receives permission of the people's authority to run the estate until Rosenberg returns from the concentration camps, or until the complete liberation of the country!

British admiral Bertram Ramsay dies in a plane crash!

The Soviet Union recognizes the Lublin Committee and the provisional government of Poland!

Tomorrow continues the distribution of flour at the Village Hall!

Notified!

In general, people like familiarity, and so they were happy to have Kalman Gubica back. They had gathered regularly at Kalman's crossroads since the start of the war; they all wanted to know at least something of what was going on, but almost no one had the money to buy the newspaper. They were not terribly bothered by Kalman's reputation as "the one who talks to himself"; Siga had seen all sorts of people, and, as long as they were not raving lunatics, they were accepted. It went without saying that, more so than ever, Kalman would enjoy their respect—not because of the man but because of the battle.

Already in the first few days of their cohabitation, the couple faced problems in getting around. How to show Mariya around Siga and its surroundings, when she only had one leg? On crutches they would only get to the end of the street; it was useless trying to go farther, since Mariya's armpits were already smarting from the sticks. It would have been logical to think about a horse and cart, but where to get one in such desperate times? The army had taken most of the horses, and those that remained were guarded like gold dust. Kalman suddenly thought of Father Matiša—he always had two horses and a wagon at his disposal—so one morning he set off to see the priest. Matiša was delighted to see Kalman, receiving him warmly and asking him about everything. He was happy to hear that Kalman had brought back a woman. But when it came to the horse, the priest paused to think. It wasn't really fitting to parade around on a horse-drawn wagon in such times. And he had only just managed to save his two horses from the army. They'd left them with him because of his service. But then he waved a hand and admonished himself quietly: he could take them for a little ride, they deserved it after all! Matiša told Kalman that he'd have the horses harnessed straight away; they could have a chat, and he could get to know Mariya. And so it was: Mariya got to see Siga in its frozen, January edition, which she liked, before spending a pleasant evening back at the priest's home. At first, Mariya was a little suspicious of the cleric, but relaxed when she saw how much Kalman trusted him. Besides, Kalman had told her before about their illicit collaboration. Matiša had a fair bit to drink, and, though satisfied with how the war was going and despite being appointed to teach religion in the school, it was as if something was tormenting him. Politically, he was reserved, restrained. And it could be felt.

One Saturday they were visited by Jula Begečki, president of the Siga Women's Anti-Fascist Front, founded in November the previous year. Jula heard that Kalman had returned with a friend from the war, a Russian woman, so she brought them some food and came to see whether they needed anything. She invited them to Mass the next day. They would gather in the center of the village and head there together, flags and all. Kalman wasn't keen on the idea, despite his friendship with Matiša, and it was clear that Mariya was not burning with desire either. But Jula Begečki's visit was important for a whole other reason. This adroit and enterprising widow, with her headscarf, broad hips, and small head, on leaving Kalman's yard wondered—unprompted, without a word of complaint from the couple—how they would get around. When she inquired how they had solved the problem, Kalman shrugged and said, "We don't have a horse." Jula Begečki raised her forefinger importantly, said excitedly that she thought she had a solution, and disappeared down the street. She returned half an hour later with something she called a "Hungarian rickshaw." It was a cart a meter long and half a meter wide, with sides again about fifty centimeters high. It was made of wood with iron rims. At the sides stood two iron bars, like shafts, by which the cart could be fastened to some kind of vehicle. Why not—Jula surmised—to a bicycle? Kalman and Mariya were delighted with the idea, and immediately Kalman pushed Mariya in the cart to the blacksmith, told him what he needed, and ran home for his bicycle, leaving Mariya to the wonders of the Siga forge. The blacksmith made them a very smart, simple device with which they could now easily attach the cart to the frame of the bicycle and pull it. They spent the rest of that January day riding around the village in the cold and sleet until they were almost frozen, returning home to warm themselves up in the heat of that eggy light. There was no need to hurry, they decided. They should leave something for tomorrow.

Months passed, spring arrived, the war was drawing to an end, and Kalman and Mariya on her bicycle cart had become a village attraction of sorts. At least in the beginning, since people get used to all sorts. Mariya was very comfortable in the cart, as they had installed a seat and lined it with rags and blankets. They bought it from a Gypsy who collected such things around Batina, from the battlefield, where all sorts of wrecked vehicles were left behind. They were, as the hackneyed saying goes, the best days of their lives. Nothing was a problem; even the obligations of life and work seemed trivial. It was as if a boundless spring meadow stretched out in front of them, bursting with plants that they, like bees, had only to help themselves to. As is the nature of people, many almost certainly envied them. However, no one stood in their way, so if there were some who were envious, they did not show themselves, unless it was they who stood behind the one misfortune that often befell the couple: flat tires. Kalman would come to the rescue every time. After all, what in the great scheme of things was one flat tire on the cart or his bicycle? Sometimes, at night, when he might find himself alone on the street, he had the feeling that the shadows of those women who had besieged and pursued him before the war were there, crouching in the dark. He could not be completely sure, but he still carried a pistol with him nonetheless. God forbid. With the exception of such foreboding, for which he had no real evidence, fortune flowed unimpeded.

Hear ye, hear ye!
   Germany capitulates, war in Europe is over!
   Fighting continues in the Pacific!
   The National Liberation Committee orders that Father Matiša be given two thousand dinars a month, to be collected from the faithful as a form of surtax!
   Notified!

The Local People's Committee (as the village authorities were now called) quickly began goading Kalman about when he planned to marry and make an honest woman of his Russian. Kalman had heard somewhere people talking of marriage as bourgeois nonsense, so he said the same.

   "It would be best if you would marry. You're not a man until you do," said Marko Karajkov, who was the clerk at the time.

"What if she doesn't want to?" asked Kalman, giving away what he really feared.

That's when Marko Karajkov offered himself as savior, telling Kalman he had something for him and inviting him to his house. When they got there, he took Kalman into the backyard, where he was immediately surrounded by five three-month-old wet-nosed puppies.

"You take her one of these shaggy things, and watch how she marries you," said Karajkov.

The man was half-genuine in his intention to help Kalman, but the other half simply wanted the hungry puppies off his hands. He was not the kind to take a log to the litter as soon as they were born, whacking them over their heads and burying them in the garden. So he was left to hand them off where he could. Kalman, however, immediately grasped the potential of the idea, took one of the puppies in his arms, thanked Karajkov, and set off all aglow.

"Sobaka!" Mariya cried out in delight when she caught sight of the dog. She wept alarmingly for the first fifteen minutes, hugging and kissing the puppy; perhaps it was the war, who could tell? Kalman grew worried and began seriously questioning whether it had been the right move in the context of his planned proposal. But when she had calmed down, when he saw that she was really very happy, Kalman began to stammer, to shift his feet, give little coughs, puff and pant. Now she grew worried, wondering, as an unfinished medical student, whether he was suffering some kind of seizure. But once he sat down and composed himself a little, the marriage proposal somehow fell from between his dry lips. Mariya grew serious. Quiet. She said that it was a matter of great consequence and

IVAN VIDAK

should be given careful thought. Clearly, it was not communicated in the most elegant fashion; they were still getting to know each other's language. But everything was understood. Kalman found her earnestness quite discouraging.

His face, in solidarity with hers, took on a look of distress. Mariya sat down next to him. She was sorry it had turned out so somber. The only thing that occurred to her was to stress that she had not turned him down, but simply wished to think it over. She reminded him that she was there, in his home. What more did he need? Finally, she admitted that she had an aversion to marriage, passed on from her mother. You see, before his death, her father had been very bad at it. Marriage, that is.

"What need do we have of such vulgar conventions in this new era?" she asked.

One would not be completely mistaken for concluding that the loss of a leg had prompted in Mariya an unwillingness and repulsion when it came to things that were whole. And it was questionable whether she ever would have desired to be with a man such as Kalman, had she not felt herself so cut in two, so destroyed, even. One should not hide from this; in many instances, love begins without a firm foothold, so to say, and flows from the most unexpected of places. Up to that point, Kalman had told her many things about himself: many things, but not the most important. Now he felt the need to lay his cards on the table. It was all or nothing.

She knew only that he had survived a lightning strike and had the scars to prove it. That could not be hidden. But there was the matter of the electric phenomenon of Kalman's genitals, about which they had never mustered the courage to talk, but took the unspoken decision to accept it as a matter of fact. Now, she learned of the insufferable Voice of the father he had never met. She listened intently, not blinking, and sensed a veil lifting from her eyes and how everything was suddenly becoming clear. Which was, of course, a little paradoxical, but not without precedent, and there was actually no call for amazement. When the story intersected with her and her role in Kalman's torment, to that so special a moment in Kalman's life, she was so captivated that she found it impossible to maintain a healthy sense of perspective. Perhaps it occurred to her that Kalman might be making up things a little, creating a crazy fantasy and as special a place as possible in it for her. But those electric nights had created the space for much to be believed. In all probability, she had never really straightened out all that in her mind. By the end of Kalman's story she was completely enchanted, filled with a horror and beauty that suddenly seemed to correspond so much with her stump, which at that very moment was washed in warm puppy pee.

* * *

Hear ye, hear ye!

Atomic bomb is dropped on second Japanese city, Nagasaki! Thousands dead!

Soviet troops attack Japanese-occupied Manchuria!

The Local People's Committee cancels the lease with the Forest Administration. The building will go to the Purchase-Sales Cooperative!

Notified!

On August 18, 1945, Kalman Gubica and Mariya Ivanovna Lomonosov were married. They exchanged vows not in the church before Matiša but in the Village Hall, before a registrar. Kalman initially expected Matiša to marry them; it seemed obvious, and he never even contemplated otherwise. However, when he shared this with the people in the Village Hall, they dropped their gaze. They upbraided him for only recently saying marriage was bourgeois nonsense and said that he, as a member of the Party, should avoid a church wedding.

"I'm a true Party man; I haven't missed one meeting," said Kalman.

But he was told that the Party was the Party and should be respected. Let Matiša do his job, hold Mass, marry people, give religious lessons in school, but members of the Party—they repeated over and over—had no place being in church. Old Panta, who was made a kind of caretaker at the Village Hall in order to put food on his table, tried to ease Kalman's discontent by asking whether he was sure that "his missus" even wanted to get married in a Catholic church. Even if she were not a communist, she'd be Orthodox. What would she be doing in our church?

"Er, yes, quite right," Kalman agreed.

But he nevertheless felt a pang of guilt, so that same day he went, very contritely, to see Father Matiša, toward whom he felt a certain debt, a friendship of the kind he had never had before, and explained everything to him. Matiša didn't particularly like it, but neither did he express any dissatisfaction.

He smiled and held out his hand. "Am I at least invited as a guest?" he joked, to which Kalman nodded with great gusto and gripped his hand.

Even had there not just been a war, it was unlikely that Kalman would have a big wedding. Certainly not of the kind parents most often organized for their children, or rather for the whole village, only to spend the rest of their lives recovering from the cost. Instead, a little after midday that August 18, Kalman and Mariya sat on their bicycle and cart, which had been lavishly decorated for the occasion, and set off for the Village Hall. Everyone they passed on the street waved at them happily, as if hailing the village crazies rather than a young couple off to get married. In the Village Hall, about fifteen people had gathered. A few work colleagues from the Hall, old and new, two young men who were also wounded at Batina, Ivica Patarić, and a certain Genge who was wounded in the final days of the battle. Father Matiša was there too, as were Marijanović, Pašić, and Škarica, and a handful of others who had been with Kalman in the forest in the days before the liberation of Siga. Kalman had those few distant relatives, but he hadn't kept in touch, and nor had they with him. The couple sat so that Mariya would not have to struggle with standing, but apart from that it was all pretty much standard fare. Happy, charming even.

At Kalman's insistence, the celebration was held in the Tench, which was now run by Öcsike's relative, István. The tavern had put the grim, subdued war years behind it, and life was slowly returning. From somewhere people found the means to pay off at least part of their debts, and more and more began stopping by the tavern. But there were no more boats on the small Danube, just two old mills and a barge for transporting wood. Life around the tavern would never return to its former glory. But no one despaired; the atmosphere was idyllic, and the wedding reception exceeded everyone's expectations. Stipan Vidak's "band" played; István made sure there was a decent amount of fish, which could still be procured; and the Village Hall provided enough wine and rakija for everyone, pulling it off somehow by issuing new drinks licenses (since for a time the inns were closed). There were also a handful of people in the Tench that Kalman knew from his days on the water, and so the happy company grew to about twenty people. They might not have known it, but inside they were thirsty for enjoyment. The war had done what war does, turned everything on its head, and, with the exception of those who had married as a reason to make merry, no one during the war had allowed themselves much chance to let off steam. It was not the first drinking session since the war, but it was the merriest, and more than any other it managed to emulate that euphoria and barroom excitement that sometimes, on special occasions, sweeps people up. In the end, everyone except Kalman was drunk. Even Mariya grew flushed sitting in her chair, laughing and forgetting briefly about all of the misery she had witnessed and experienced. At one end of the arranged tables, a drunk Matiša and Marijanović sat and talked; at the other end, Pašić and Škarica howled to the tamburitza; some, carried away by drink, even arm wrestled, others ate as much as they could, while a few passed out, heads on the table. Sometime after midnight, Kalman and Mariya bade a fond farewell to the guests, received one more loud and warm congratulations, and rode home.

From the wedding onward their love only grew. "Moy sumasshedshiy elektricheskiy chelovek," Mariya would tell Kalman, gazing at him from her floating, yellow trance. The two of them resembled morphine addicts, one moment smiling absently to themselves in some self-satisfied ecstasy, the next smiling at each other like good-natured calves. They would quietly observe each other, exchanging the occasional expression of adoration and deep affection. Mariya had few variations: held aloft by the opiate light, she turned in the air like some kind of cosmonaut, naked and bathed in sweat. Kalman's postcoital trance, on the other hand, had various incarnations, from sitting to lying to standing limply against the wall; one day he cried, the next he roared with laughter, the day after that he just breathed and observed. The one constant in that whole spectrum of experiences was the all-permeating and healing satisfaction—even when he cried, he did so happily. Sumasshedshiy elektricheskiy chelovek.

Sobaka stayed Sobaka. They never gave her a new name, because Kalman liked this one. She was small, roughly ten kilograms, covered in long, curly fur. A quiet and well-tempered dog that never exhibited any of the neuroses or fixations that afflicted old Toza. Sobaka liked her yard; even the gate accidentally left open was not a temptation. She liked to eat, to bury bones, to chew logs, and to hunt rodents. She was not fond of cats. She adored sleep. Only when in heat would she press her nose to the gate, but not even then would she run away, and the young couple never had any trouble with her. A few times Kalman put her in the bicycle cart in order to take her with him on his work round, thinking after all that she should probably spend a little time outside the yard. But she would jump out as soon as he started pedaling, run back to the gate, and wait for him to open it for her. By postwar village standards, Mariya's little sweetheart was an unusually fat dog.

In the autumn of 1948, Mariya discovered that she was pregnant. There was no limit to the excitement Kalman felt at the prospect of becoming a father. It began as a general euphoria that simply went on and on. He couldn't sit still and barely slept. Especially now, when, due to the new circumstances, it was decided there would be no sex for the time being, a state of affairs that terrified Kalman. He bought everyone drinks and told the news even to strangers. Then he was left a little unoccupied, unsure what to do with himself. They began fishing together, but it didn't last long, as Kalman felt he wanted some time alone. Mariya showed endless understanding for him and his reaction, since she knew how unsettled and, to a degree, traumatic his life had been. It was then that Kalman took it upon himself to put the house and yard in order, replacing the reeds on the roof and anything inside or outside the house that wobbled, creaked, or was prone to sticking. Something, some kind of restlessness, drove him to Father Matiša too. Matiša already knew everything and was happy to see him. That veiled dissatisfaction on the priest's face had somehow deepened, due to the fact that much of the church's land had been swept up in the agrarian reform. But Matiša would say with a gentle smile and wide-open arms, "If that's the worst that can happen..." Kalman was terribly torn, he told Matiša— should the child be baptized? Hounded by that fear of God that afflicts poor men, Kalman felt he was not a good communist. Matiša continued smiling, almost entertained by the question, and told him that, if he were to decide on a baptism, the new parish priest would have to perform it, since he was moving on; it was time.

"Ah," said Kalman, throwing his arms wide the same as Matiša had done a moment before. "Then it's not important."

Kalman felt great affection for Matiša. How could he not, when the man had been such a big part of his life for six years, six of the most intense and profound years ever? What's more, this man of the cloth always had understanding and a good word for Kalman, even when he got on his nerves. They parted a little awkwardly, without a real farewell, since Kalman had always had a fear of saying goodbye to those he cared for.

"Good... Well, see you then," he said, as if they would see each other many times more before Matiša would leave.

Warmly, but quietly, Matiša replied, "See you, dear Kalman."

That was the last time they saw one another. Twenty years later, Matiša would become the first bishop of Subotica. As parish priest in Siga he was replaced by Marko Kovačev, whom Kalman did not properly meet. He avoided the church, considering it from that moment somehow always empty, and he hardly even knew the sound of the new priest's voice. With Matiša's departure, Kalman spent more and more time alone. It was as if that excitement in him gradually mutated, and his positive reaction to the prospect of fatherhood began to transform into restlessness that devolved into sleeplessness. After spending the whole night awake, tossing and turning, Kalman would leave for work in the morning without a word and would not return until the evening. He would slip into a grove by some water and consider, deeply and with growing concern, everything that might happen to him, tormenting himself with unnecessary fantasies. He grew quieter still, tenser, scratching at his head with more and more worry. Initially,

Mariya left him alone, finding understanding for things for which there should be none. She endured like that for a few months before she began seriously worrying about him. She felt increasingly alone, and abandoned.

It happened one sunny day on the eve of summer. A new wave of tension washing over him, Kalman was fishing from a riverbank, or rather staring at the water completely unaware of the float on the surface, when the Voice returned. At first, Kalman was struck dumb when he realized that the tension was making his hands clench. Then he heard him, as loud and clear as the first time. But the terror that gripped him was many times greater than the first time, as if that had not been terrifying enough! This new terror was made more intense by the knowledge of what he had already lived through with the Voice, and everything that experience had brought with it. So the terror was multiplied by the awareness of all that awaited him. However, because of Mariya's pregnancy, Kalman after all had a little more strength, enough that he resolved to fight. This time he would not buckle, he would not surrender, he would not engage in conversation with the Voice. He vowed not to say a word to him. Never. May he fall down dead or burst into flames if he ever broke the promise. Nevertheless, circumstances quickly reminded him of what he should have known already: resisting the Voice was no easy matter. And so a few hours later he was in the Tench, knocking back rakija like it was water. István watched him worriedly, repeatedly refilling his glass, until Kalman took the bottle out of his hands and began pouring it for himself. At a corner table two old boozers sniggered, pleased with the return of their old chum. Kalman did his work for the day but returned to the Tench in the evening and finished the bottle, drinking until he passed out and fell on the floor half-dead. István had no way to carry him home, and so Kalman once more spent the night on the floor; he woke in the morning with the first rays of sun and headed home. Mariya immediately caught the smell of alcohol. She knew very well what alcohol did to people, having long been surrounded by them, and undoubtedly Kalman's sobriety played a big part in her agreement to marry him. She said nothing, preparing his breakfast in silence and hoping that he was simply extremely worried, a little pathologically, yes, but hardly unheard of, she thought. Everything would be fine; best let him work it out himself. Kalman, however, had no other solution but self-medication. So the days began to blur into one, like a monotone reflection in a mirror. Mariya was concerned first and foremost for the child inside her, who was supposed to enter the world in November, while Kalman became withdrawn and drank insatiably.

One day, undoubtedly because of the terrible things that the Voice was saying to him, Kalman stopped coming home altogether. He went to work and spent the rest of the day and night in the Tench; he was so drunk he barely finished his evening round on his feet. Sometimes, several times a day, he drank himself unconscious, collapsing on the table, and, after a short sleep, drank himself into oblivion once more. In order to stabilize the bicycle beneath him, he stopped taking off the cart, so it was always attached. Sometimes he would fall asleep drunk in the street, sitting on Mariya's seat. One morning, several young men on their way to work found him like that, so one of them sat on the bicycle and rode him back to his house, leaving him outside. But Kalman woke before Mariya spotted him and fled to the Tench, in order to "compose himself" before the morning round. Then, after he had failed to come home for days on end, Mariya tracked him down at the Village Hall and confronted him, asking what on earth was going on. The poor woman was by now quite desperate. And one should not make the mistake of thinking that Kalman was indifferent toward her and her situation; it pained him considerably, but that was all drowned out inside him by the Voice, which was so intense it simply left no room for any feeling or thought inside Kalman to be articulated in full, except those that the Voice itself provoked. While Mariya tolerated him, he could just about get by—if it could be called getting by—but when she called him to account, the pressure became unbearable; he could no longer cope with the vice he was in.

Hear ye, hear ye!

The Communist Information Bureau continues to slander our country and leadership!

Comrade Tito and his comrades firmly respond! Among other things it was said: "The Central Committee of the Communist Party of Yugoslavia invites the party membership to close ranks in the struggle to achieve the party's aims and for even stronger unity within the Party, and calls on the working class and other working masses, gathered together in the People's Front, to work even harder in the building of our Socialist homeland. That is the only path and the only means to demonstrate in practice the injustice of the mentioned accusations."

The first postwar census in Siga has been completed. Siga has 4,555 residents. There are 3,443 Croats, 160 Serbs, four Montenegrins,

three Bulgarians, eight Russians, two Albanians, 178 Romanians,
15 Roma, 694 Hungarians, six Czechs, five Slovenes, two Muslims,
three Rusyns, 27 Germans, 27 Italians and five others!
  Notified!

A skeptic might be forgiven for thinking that it was the Voice's idea. But it was not. It was all Kalman's doing. One sweltering July day, all grimy, snotty, red-eyed, pee-soaked, and stinking, Kalman met Pera, the state security spook from Sombor, at the Village Hall. Pera would visit the Village Hall a few times a week to talk about the situation and collect information, particularly now when matters with the Soviets had escalated. This balding, chubby, and actually well-meaning man was well-known in Siga, having lived and worked there before the war as a day laborer for almost all the big landowners. Now he was an officer of the secret police covering Siga. A few years later he would be transferred to another post as wholly unreliable, given his fondness for eating and drinking and his lack of stomach for serious matters of the state. This was the Pera that Kalman met and told him, all stern and red in the face, that something had to be done about his wife.

"She's Russian, a Red Army woman, and she won't stop talking about Stalin. She keeps saying how the Soviets will show us what's what." And what she says about our leaders, Kalman dared not even repeat.

Pera knew Kalman and that, though before he was known to talk to himself in the street, he was now a serious man, a fighter. So he looked at him, surprised, his eyebrows raised.

"Are you absolutely sure, comrade?" Pera asked.

"Absolutely. Take her away. She'll have all our heads!"

After the war, a station of the People's Militia had been set up in Siga, so Pera sat in his jeep and went to fetch two officers. In the meantime, Kalman jumped on his bicycle and sped home. He found Mariya in the yard by the well, hanging washing out to dry. He left the bicycle in the street, ran into the yard all breathless, and grabbed his wife by the shoulder. She was actually pleased to see him, since he had not come home for so long, and she had been thinking about how it really made no sense anymore and something would have to be done. She didn't know what, but something!

"Mariya," he said, "my love, my everything..."

Mariya thought that he had come to his senses.

"My father, the Voice... You remember, I told you? He's come back! He's come back, and for you too, for both of you," he said, taking her hand and placing it on her belly. "There's no room for you here anymore. It's too dangerous. You have to leave right away!"

Mariya managed to understand him perfectly, but she expected him to say something else, something more. So she let out a disappointed sigh and returned to the laundry. For the first time it truly occurred to her that she had made a mistake in staying with him. She should have gone home, to Vladivostok, to her mother.

"Mariya," Kalman mumbled, almost choking on the words. "Forgive me. Wherever they take you, it'll be better for you and the child than staying here."

At that moment, Pera and two militia officers entered the yard. Mariya paused and looked at Kalman.

"What have you done?"

Pera eyed Kalman standing next to the poor one-legged woman with child and asked, "Are you completely sure?" With both hands he pointed with pity at the visibly scared woman.

Kalman nodded and looked away cowardly. Pera signaled with his head to the militia officers and, full of sympathy, told Mariya, "Don't resist, comrade. Everything will be fine. Don't worry. We're just going to have a talk."

As the two militia officers took Mariya by the arms, Pera shouted at them to go easy on her. Mariya did not struggle, but her eyes, filled with disbelief, bore desperately into Kalman.

"What did you tell them, Kalman? What is this? Where are they taking me? Why, Kalman?" Then she broke down in a flood of tears through which she could barely breathe, let alone speak. When they had placed her in the jeep and turned on the engine, right before they drove away, she let out a terrifying scream: "Kalman!"

His head bowed, Kalman closed the gate behind him as the sound of the jeep's engine grew quieter and quieter.

The pursuit of Communist Information Bureau sympathizers would hot up only later, particularly the following year. Though Mariya was among the first to be arrested in the former Yugoslavia, no one else in Siga was ever arrested for the same reason. Clearly, arrests were occasionally made on other grounds, but no one else because of the resolution issued in June 1948 that expelled the Communist Party of Yugoslavia, accusing it of deviating from Marxist Leninism.

IVAN VIDAK

And so Siga, as before the war, drifted back into its distinct, peaceful, and remote existence, far removed from the wider world and its dramatic goings-on.

Hear ye, hear ye!

President Ivan Karajkov asks the peasant workers' cooperative for 50 kilograms of flour, so that the women can lay on a celebration to see in the new year of 1949!

It is concluded that the preventive spraying against mosquitoes in 1948 was successfully executed!

In the space of ten months, game warden Ivan Kaplar caught 34 badgers, from which he made soap. Some of the badgers weighed up to 20 kilograms!

Notified!

7.

EVIL, BUT WORSE, the worst. Such was Kalman's reputation now. Everyone soon found out what he had done and how. All they didn't know was why, but that was less interesting, and only the most curious might occasionally discuss it in passing. It's difficult to say whether that alone was the reason for the new indifference to his news bulletins, since it might anyway have been expected of the people of Siga, given that the war was over. But certainly it did not help. That said, no one at the Village Hall gave even a passing thought to punishing Kalman, since from the perspective of those in power he was loyal, deserving of praise, not to mention a fighter, as if that could never be stressed enough. But it was obvious and could be felt even among his colleagues at the Hall: people steered clear of him, and no one wanted anything to do with him beyond what was required. They said hello, on the surface they remained courteous, but, interestingly, no one smiled at him. In fact, above all, people feared him. Who would not fear an impenetrable and mercurial man in a position of power? Might he report me as a Stalinist too? they wondered. Only from the drunks in the Tench could he hear words of friendship and warmth, though it's well-known that drunks live by a completely different set of rules.

By God, not even Kalman was the same. Since he had sent Mariya on her way, it was as if he had found peace of sorts. And not because the Voice had disappeared or anything in that sense had changed, but as a reaction to a situation more extreme than extreme: the Voice had not so much been a threat to him, as much as to his pregnant wife, and now, with her gone, it was as if the Voice was far easier to handle. So nothing had changed in the Voice, but Kalman had been so scared for Mariya and their unborn child that their removal from his field of vision felt, on his nerves, like a slingshot stretched to the breaking point had suddenly been relaxed. Kalman felt he had done the right thing. This does not mean he was not conscious of the horror of his act, but that the alternative may have been far worse. Which, he alone knew. We should believe him, if we can. It was as if his worry for Mariya and the child had made room for itself inside him, so when that worry was gone, a gap was left. A fair-sized gap, like a pair of baggy trousers. Like bare feet in the hot summer air, when army boots are removed after days of marching. And so now, thanks to Mariya and a bizarre twist of fate, he was able to cope with the Voice far more easily than before. He did not waver from the promise he made to himself that he would not exchange a word with him ever again. And whereas before that dialogue with his unseen father brought relief—and ignoring that torrent of words and demands was

IVAN VIDAK

intolerable—now everything was the other way around. It's no miracle that someone who feared snakes might now, soaked in experience and spite, become a hunter of snakes, right? That he who was beaten as a boy should now beat others. That a blacksmith, who was left with bloody blisters from the hammer on the first day of his apprenticeship, now pulls live coals from the fire with his bare hands. And so too Kalman learned to live with the Voice over the years that followed. As if he had compartmentalized him, put him in a corner. It was not at all as easy as it might sound; Kalman had to resort to many tricks, most notably a kind of incomprehensible mumbling that he gradually developed. His lips worked without pause, an inarticulate, quiet hum that would spread from his mouth as from a distant mill on the Danube. A rumbling torrent out of which, here and there, would surface the odd discernible word, this time in Serbo-Croat (deer... communists... Hungarian sympathizers... you damn...), but not enough to make any sense of it—like a book in which the reader reads only one word on each page. That mumbling eased his anxiety and helped him to exist independently, to develop his own voice, so to say. And, of course, there was the daily intoxication. It was no longer so frantic. Instead, Kalman constantly maintained a certain level of drunkenness, which allowed him to function and meant he no longer embarrassed himself with all sorts of drunken excesses, despite drinking constantly. Undoubtedly another manifestation of maturity and experience.

He was done with sex. Although he might be tempted by the opportunities that continued to present themselves from the dark, he would resist, until he finally decided, in honor of

Mariya and his unfortunate child, that it just wouldn't do. He felt like he would be spitting on a victim, on love. Since, in spite of everything, for Kalman that love had not ended. As far as he was concerned, he was still a married man. That would never change. And his marriage continued, despite, in Kalman's eyes, objective circumstances that meant they could not be together. Kalman knew that Mariya would never be able to understand. Hence celibacy. Although, to settle his rage, it would have done him good to roll around with one of those corpulent figures from the dark, out of spite, before the imagined eyes of the Voice. He had no use for shame; he would hand it off to the Voice. But hey, in celibacy he found a last drop of dignity, a last monument to his beloved wife, an act of fidelity. What a fool.

Nevertheless, there was one creature devoted to Kalman Gubica. After Mariya's departure, Sobaka's behavior changed dramatically. At first tied to the house, the yard, and Mariya, the dog was left confused by the sudden disappearance of her mistress. That quiet little dog spent days patiently waiting, and then one day walked up to Kalman and jumped into the Hungarian rickshaw, from which she had fled before. Just like that, she jumped in, as if it was part of her everyday routine, sat down, and looked calmly at Kalman. This so warmed his heart that he smiled. And from that moment Sobaka never left his side. Calm and good-tempered, like Toza, but without the fixations that in the end delineated the strange spiritual life of that dog. Sobaka was so easygoing that she radiated calm around her, like a kind of talisman. Kalman was good to her, fed her regularly, and did not neglect her, as had been his tendency at times with Toza. This improved his image by the slightest degree, but nevertheless not enough to put things right and for most people to stop avoiding him. Kalman had little concern for his image; for him, the loyalty and kindness of his young dog were enough.

And that's how Kalman spent the years after 1948. In 1950, he moved house: voluntarily, he gave up his home to a settler family from Kordun in exchange for a small fisherman's house in the direct vicinity of the Tench, and in which the fairly large family had been temporarily and quite inadequately housed. It was a single room with a bed and a small table. The windows were broken, the insides were ruined, and the thatched roof was seriously damaged. But the authorities fixed it all from the public purse, since, after all, the house Kalman gave up had been worth more. He would spend the rest of his life in that space of ten square meters, like some kind of hermit.

Hear ye, hear ye!

Deep winter plowing has been carried out on 1,103 acres, of which 723 private, 328 cooperative, and 142 house lots.

Five boars brought from Kosovo, let out in Kazuk and Kalandoš, which will help boost the current stock that was decimated by the war.

Construction starts on power line from Bezdan to Siga. Electricity next year!

Notified!

In 1953, work began on bringing electricity to Siga. That whole summer, Kalman rode his bicycle on the road to Bezdan and watched how the power line was strung. He felt a strange excitement. He would stand at the side of the road and spend two, three hours observing the workers sweating in the scorching summer sun. They began saying things, goading him, even insulting him, but Kalman would not budge. A few times, some of the workers tried to approach him, but Sobaka would let out a growl and briefly but gruffly bark at them to make them pull back. When he had satisfied his curiosity for the day, Kalman would quietly sit back on his bicycle and go about his own business. While the transmission line was still being strung, the construction of the House of Culture was completed. It was a large building with a hall that could accommodate several hundred people and a host of smaller rooms for various purposes. On the first floor, with windows looking onto the street, onto the center of Siga and the church, was the room which, so they said, would be Kalman's new place of work. A public address system had already been delivered, and twelve speakers were mounted on the top of the electricity pylons in the village itself, at those crossroads where Kalman had banged his drum. And when the power line was finally finished, Kalman's job was transformed. One spring morning in 1954, the electricity was turned on in Siga to great festivity, with a ceremony in the center of the village, music, and barbecued meat and stew cooked over open fires. Kalman's voice rang out from the speakers, which at that moment were all that was electrified in Siga, at least until the evening, when the streetlights were turned on. He announced the participants in the event, hosted guests in his little studio, and was particularly proud when one of them dubbed his new workplace "Radio Siga."

Radio was not unfamiliar to him, because for a few years already there had been a foreign radio receiver in the Village Hall on which they could listen to a whole host of broadcasts.

Powered by generator, of course. Kalman felt important, promoted, special. In the days after the celebration, the radio receiver was installed in his "studio," and the radio broadcasts were played over the speakers between Kalman's news bulletins. In general, he stayed in the House of Culture, interrupting the programs from elsewhere with the odd witty remark, but at least once a day he would go to the electricity substation on the western edge of Siga, near the cemetery, and listen in. For right at the beginning, in the first days after the arrival of electricity, Kalman had discovered an unusual sound inside the substation. That tall, thin, windowless, towerlike construction had a heavy metal door on which someone had clumsily painted a red lightning bolt. Kalman had initially been drawn to that drippy symbol, but when he got closer he heard a distinct sound, like cascading water, the fine crackle of electricity, and became completely hypnotized. For several hours at a time, he would sit and lean his back against the door or with his ear pressed to it. Mumbling his incoherent mantra, this unusual man would seem to people even wilder, one moment planted beside the building, a crazed look in his eye, the next moment screaming over the speakers. Sometimes they would see him at the substation at night too, under the streetlights. This was a particularly scary sight, given that the nighttime lighting had come as a shock to the people of Siga. After centuries of darkness, everything was visible at night now, as if the entire world they knew had fled from the light in search of darkness elsewhere. Truly, with the coming of electricity, Siga had become a whole different place entirely.

Kalman too had moments when he despaired at the disappearance of night, but the power and freshness that electricity brought to other aspects of life went some way to diminishing that suffering. True, earlier there had been those few lamps in the center of Siga that were lit by the generator, but the effect was insignificant when most of the village was still in darkness. Sombor hospital was also illuminated by electricity at that time, but that was not Kalman's natural habitat, and, particularly in those days of peace, it had no real impact on his life. Electricity was also brought to his new house, but for some reason Kalman never bought bulbs and intentionally left his home in darkness, or lit only by candle. The biggest shock was the lights in the Tench: instead of candles and lamps, there blazed electric sunlight from the ceiling, so even that remote corner of Siga was not spared the great changes. Guests who had appreciated the dark ambience stopped coming and were replaced by new ones. Despite his enthusiasm for electricity, Kalman stayed away from the inns, confirming without a doubt that illuminated nightlife was not for him. He drank his evening rakija in front of his own home, in the company of Sobaka, in the dark.

The first few months were exciting. Opening the window of his studio, Kalman would hear his own voice right there, on the crossroads, along the street that ran between the House of Culture and the church. In his drunken head, he multiplied that twelve times and imagined the polyphonic resonance of his voice echoing from the speakers: invisible, powerful, important. It was then, however, that a series of unfortunate events began to unfold, events that would determine Kalman's fate. It started with the death of Sobaka. Not even the veterinarian Kalman called to help (which was rare, given that almost nobody called out the veterinarian because of a dog) had no idea what the problem was. He said it might have something to do with ticks, which made sense, given that all village dogs were regularly full of them, and people only pulled them off when they had inflated to the size of peas and were clearly visible. Sobaka was six and a half years old, which at that time was the average lifespan of a dog. She lay there listless, refusing food and water, her breathing quick and her eyes staring ahead, blinking worriedly. The veterinarian said nothing could be done. "Call a huntsman." But Kalman did not have the strength. He laid the dog on a folded blanket, placed food and water on the floor beside her, and hurried home every evening from the House of Culture. He wanted to be with her when she went, to see her off in the way he had never had the chance with anyone dear to him. But even that eluded him: Sobaka died one afternoon while Kalman was at work. He found her at rest and still warm, the tip of her tongue peeking from her mouth. He began flogging himself with the thought that he would have been with her had howling from the speakers not, after all, been more important.

Coming to understand oneself is always sad. Kalman did not often cry. It was unusually rare, in fact, considering his nature. He had cried a little in the early days of the Voice and then during the war. True, a few times out of love as well. And now he cried. But differently, not so snottily, sobbing and uncontrollable, but quietly, warmly, almost tenderly. He lay beside Sobaka, stroked her on her side and head, still mumbling, but gently, measuredly, and devotedly. At that moment, in a tiny fraction of one moment, Kalman had the feeling he saw the meaning of all life: death. He had seen so much death, so many spent fates, that it seemed to him that life was nothing else but death, that there was always as much death as life, and that it was so omnipresent and close that it was perhaps a little inappropriate and tasteless to lament it at all. He buried Sobaka behind his little fisherman's house, removed the cart from his bicycle, and left it on the grave as a monument, so it wouldn't get wet. It was another painful but altogether different experience. Perhaps because Sobaka did not speak, who knows?

The second in that chain of events occurred a few months later, right before winter, with the visit of Pera the Spook. Kalman was in the House of Culture; he had just announced that in the middle of December the House would host the Hunter's Ball, a merry and sumptuous affair (Sanyika Varga, president of the hunting association, was with him for the announcement, with a few greatly exaggerated claims to drum up interest and get people to pay the registration fee). Kalman saw out his guest and was planning to pop briefly into the Tench for a bottle of rakija, when Pera knocked on his door. Slightly pained and wringing his hat in his hands, he greeted Kalman and asked if they could sit for a moment. Pera was tipsy and had a bottle of rakija in his pocket, so Kalman found the balm for his restlessness, pulling the bottle from Pera's pocket and taking a swig while at the same time gesturing for him to sit on the one of the stools by the address system. Kalman looked out the window at the falling snow; the evenings were drawing in, bloody winter. Pera seemed not to care that Kalman had helped himself to his bottle. He belched booze and garlic and slumped onto the stool.

"Let me tell you something, comrade," began Pera. "That wife of yours... She's in Russia now. I... You know how things worked back then, you heard? Yeah, it works like that now too.

But in the beginning, you could... And I didn't do it by myself; they told me to. Anyway, I escorted her to Bezdan, to the Hungarian border, and handed her over to the border guards. What happened next, I don't know, but here you go," said Pera, and held out a letter.

Kalman accepted the open, ragged letter, without a full address, only the words "Kalman Gubica, Siga, Yugoslavia" written in Russian, with the stamp of the Soviet Union and no return address.

"I quit a few years back. It wasn't for me. Actually, they transferred me to Customs. It's all right there. But anyway, a colleague came to see me this morning and brought this letter. Told me to take it to you. And here I am, by command. Fuck me, lucky it turned out like that. A year later and I wouldn't have been able to sleep at night. I don't know how you... Pregnant wife. Only one leg. War, eh!"

Pera belched a few more times, lit a cigarette, waved idly, and left. It was only when he had gone that Kalman realized that, besides the letter, he held in his hand Pera's bottle, a strong mulberry spirit, only half drunk. And that's how he sat, scrunching the letter in his sweaty hands and waiting for the liquid courage to ignite his blood. Finally, he steeled himself and opened the letter. It read:

Дорогой Калман Лайошевич,

мне трудно прощать, и даже если бы я могла, я не представляю, чего бы я этим добилась: мне не кажется, что ты человек, оглядывающийся назад. Вот почему я сообщаю тебе — у тебя сын. Жив, здоров, ему шесть лет, его зовут Лео. Я говорю тебе это по настоянию моей матери. Если бы это зависело от меня, ты бы больше не слышал о нас. Я скажу ему, когда он вырастет, кто его отец. Я не имею права держать такие вещи в секрете от него, какими бы они ни были.

А ты, Калман Лайошевич, ищи врача, ищи помощи, они тебе помогут.

Тем не менее, я желаю тебе всего наилучшего,
Мария Ивановна Ломоносова

Kalman didn't understand a thing, which suddenly drove him mad. But then he turned over the page and saw that one of Pera's men, in an uneven hand and with the dirty marks of a lead pencil, had carefully translated everything. He drank the rest of the bottle, turned on the address system, and after some brief feedback, began reading:

Dear Kalman,

It is hard for me to forgive, and even if I could, I don't see what it would achieve; you don't seem to me the kind of man who looks back. So I'm letting you know—you have a son. Alive, healthy, six years old, and called Lav. I'm telling you this on the insistence of my mother. If it was up to me, you would never hear from us again. I will tell him, when he comes of age, who his father is. I have no right to keep such things from him, whatever their nature.

As for you, Kalman, find a doctor, find help, it will do you good.

All the same, I wish you the best,
Mariya Ivanovna Lomonosov

IVAN VIDAK

In the cold twilight, the sound of the speakers reached the ears of the odd passerby, but by now very few paid attention to everything that came out of them. By then, Kalman uttered whatever nonsense came to his mind, but no one cared anymore. Ah, if only there was a photograph, to see my son, he thought, but Mariya had not gone that far. Understandably so.

For days, Kalman thought about the letter. It had caught him off guard, unprepared. As if peeping out from a corner and waving at him. A kind of recollection he had let go of, that he did not acknowledge. Something he had not wished to know. What had he even thought? That Mariya was in prison? And her leg? And the child? Truth be told, he hadn't given it much thought at all. He hid it from himself like some kind of family shame. Pushed it to one side like a pebble in his shoe. It existed, but did not exist. But now, there it was. Rinsed and salvaged, though no thanks to him. A son. By God, a son! Like he had once been. Once more, after who knows how many times already, Kalman was confronted with the misery of his own being. Would it ever end? Won't someone take away that mirror?

Kalman spent more and more time at the substation, listening to the hum of the electricity. If someone passed and said hello, he would whip around and glare at whoever had dared jolt him from his reverie. Occasionally, he would spend the night beside the door. Some kind soul would wake him in the morning. Kalman would come to with a start, thank them awkwardly, but nevertheless stay a little longer, listening to the electricity before heading to the House of Culture. He would stop by one of the inns, whichever, and ask for a rakija in a large glass; you see, by then his hands were shaking terribly in the mornings.

He was always more and more stained with piss and dribble, greasier and filthier, smellier and more rancid: he no longer resisted entropy.

It was the radio that finished off Kalman. Other people also played a part, as is often the way. One morning at the beginning of 1955, Ilija Begečki, then the clerk at the Village Hall, appeared at Kalman's door with a big Zagreb-made Yugoslav radio receiver. Everyone was tired of Kalman by then. They could no longer bear his tyranny on the airwaves, reporting only the news that he found interesting and commenting incessantly on the music from the receiver in the House of Culture as dangerous meddling, since who wishes to be constantly confronted by their basic emotions? Then, like now, it was the type of music that left one to conclude that man was nothing more than a slave to romantic ecstasy. Is that all there is? Kalman grew contemptuous of people, and, in the end, it was unclear who wanted whose head more. And when coupled with his disheveled appearance, there was no way that Kalman could hold on to his job.

Radio receivers, to the fortune of that long-suffering populace, had become a mass phenomenon. Practically every house-hold had one. The informational power Kalman wielded had become a thing of the past. On the radio people would hear well-founded and detailed news, not this bare-bones nonsense of Kalman's. And now they finally had a pretext to get rid of him. Ilija had brought him the radio receiver as a farewell gift, not knowing that Kalman had never consumed electricity in his own home. As you see, Kalman wasn't needed anymore. Interestingly, he did not resist. He was tired.

In the end, it happened like this: in the spring of 1955, out of the blue, there was a power cut. A siren was heard from the volunteer firefighters association, only recently installed. Besides the firefighters, a mass of people gathered at the substation, which was in flames. Sparks cascaded through the door, and small explosions rang in people's ears. Some of those gathered claimed that directly before the incident, Kalman had entered the substation. Panta, the caretaker from the Village Hall, confirmed that the keys to the structure were missing and that it was possible Kalman had taken them. The drama went on for hours, and when it was finally over and the firemen entered, there was no corpse to be found. Later, someone said that a shadow was found burned on one of the walls, black and motionless, with arms held high and wide and a magnificent erection. But no body. And if that was not strange enough, from that day on, Kalman could not be found. It was as if the ground had opened up and swallowed him. But before life in Siga returned to normal, another bizarre curiosity occurred.

Residents were reluctant to recall what happened, but that does not diminish the truth of it. The same day as the fire in the substation, the twelve speakers in Siga, which had not been functioning since Kalman Gubica had been pushed out, suddenly began working again. The first thing that could be heard was the hum of electricity, similar to the sound outside the substation, and then, later, barking began. A long, persistent, and loud bark over the veil of electricity. A bark that did not cease. The bark of an enraged dog, hoarse at times, desperate and bloody, shameless and denuded. The bark of a chained-up, battered dog. The villagers at first did not understand what was going on, until darkness fell, and, in the still of night, things became clearer. There was no electricity because the substation was destroyed, and it was said that the repair would take weeks, providing the parts could be found quickly. But that bark went on and on, despite the paradoxical fact that there was no electricity and it was completely impossible. Before dawn, people gathered at each of the twelve speakers, called the militia, and over the next hour or so, each one was cut from the power line with axes. Falling to the ground, they continued to bark until one by one the speakers were hacked to pieces. The remains were tossed onto a great bonfire in the middle of the village near the House of Culture, next to the memorial plaque to those who fell in Batina. The villagers gathered at the bonfire. To make sure. Those of weaker nerves cried; those of a stronger constitution comforted them. But everyone was happy that it was quiet, that the speakers were no more. The fire lit up every face.

About Sandorf Passage

SANDORF PASSAGE publishes work that creates a prismatic perspective on what it means to live in a globalized world. It is a home to writing inspired by both conflict zones and the dangers of complacency. All Sandorf Passage titles share in common how the biggest and most important ideas are best explored in the most personal and intimate of spaces.